Dear Reader,

Our grandfather, the author Willard Price, is famous for his *Adventure Stories for Boys* series, which he began writing in 1949. The series is set across fourteen stories in which the intrepid brothers Hal and Roger Hunt travel to faraway locations, where they find themselves in scorching deserts, the freezing Arctic, dense jungles and deep in the sea.

Thousands of readers have followed the brothers as they travelled the world in search of exotic animals for zoos, and have been introduced to new cultures and people through these stories. Of course, we must remember that, back then, searching for animals for zoos was a forward-thinking, conservationist approach to saving rare species, and a way to teach people about endangered habitats. The language used by Roger and Hal to describe people of other countries and customs was appropriate at the time of writing, and reflects a period when very little was known about different cultures.

So, where did our grandfather get his inspiration for his stories? Now, you see, Grandpa Price was a pioneer traveller himself – over a period of sixty years he visited one hundred and forty-eight countries. Of course, he travelled at a time when the aeroplane was just being invented, when people communicated by letter or telegraph, and so he travelled by motor car, ship, horse, and even by elephant and camel – there were few places on Earth that he wouldn't visit. He had many wonderful adventures, some of which may very well be in the story that you are about to read . . .

We are so pleased that you are about to embark on an adventure with the wise Hal and the impulsive Roger, and we wish you luck as you search with them for unusual wildlife and great adventure.

The grand daughters of Willard Price:

Katharine Price
Susannah Price Haney
Rebecca Price Brooks

WILLARD PRICE

AMAZON ADVENTURE

RED FOX

AMAZON ADVENTURE
A RED FOX BOOK 978 0 099 48226 0

First published in Great Britain by Jonathan Cape, Ltd
An imprint of Random House Children's Publishers UK
A Random House Group Company

Jonathan Cape edition published 1951
Red Fox edition published 1993
This edition published 2012

5 7 9 10 8 6 4

Penguin Random House is committed to a sustainable future for
our business, our readers and our planet. This book is made from
Forest Stewardship Council® certified paper.

MIX
Paper from
responsible sources
FSC® C018179

Printed and bound in Great Britain by Clays Ltd, St Ives plc

Red Fox Books are published by Random House Children's Publishers UK
61–63 Uxbridge Road, London W5 5SA

www.randomhousechildrens.co.uk
www.totallyrandombooks.co.uk
www.randomhouse.co.uk

Addresses for companies within The Random House Group Limited can be
found at: www.randomhouse.co.uk/offices.htm

THE RANDOM HOUSE GROUP Limited Reg. No. 954009

A CIP catalogue record for this book is available from the British Library.

For Jonathan

By the same author:

South Sea Adventure
Arctic Adventure
Safari Adventure
Elephant Adventure
Underwater Adventure
Lion Adventure
Gorilla Adventure
Whale Adventure
Tiger Adventure
African Adventure
Diving Adventure
Cannibal Adventure
Volcano Adventure

AMAZON ADVENTURE

Contents

1	The Mysterious Cablegram	1
2	The Following Shoes	8
3	Dawn Flight	16
4	Headhunters	25
5	The Condor's Shadow	37
6	The Face on the Trail	51
7	Jungle Night	60
8	Down the Dotted Line	70
9	The Chase	80
10	Mystery of the Vampire Bat	93
11	Noah's Ark on the Amazon	108
12	Disaster	126
13	Escape	132
14	Bucking Bronco Crocodile	148
15	Great Snakes!	156
16	Bullets at Midnight	174
17	Wrestling Match	187
18	Go West, Young Man	196
19	Tiger Comes to Call	207
20	Tigers Take No Nonsense	217
21	Tiger by the Tail	230
22	Black Beauty	240
23	Giant Anaconda	249
24	Nine Headless Men	266

25	Deserted	270
26	The Floating Island	285
27	The Caged Man	310

1
The Mysterious Cablegram

Hal sat on the head of a stuffed crocodile in the lobby of the Quito Hotel and cleaned his gun. He listened to the hotel proprietor, Don Pedro.

"Yes, you're going to see the greatest river on earth . . . the greatest unexplored jungle on earth . . . greatest storehouse of natural resources on earth. Some day the Amazon will feed the world."

"But are there really crocs down there as big as this one?" asked Hal, who was more interested in hunting than in feeding the world.

"Bigger. You've come to the right place if you want to get animals for the zoos. Why, I've heard say there are more varieties of wild animals in the Amazon country than in the rest of the world put together. But you'd know better about that." He turned to Hal's father.

People had a habit of turning to John Hunt when they wanted to learn about animals. He had studied and collected animals for twenty years. When Mollie the lion died at the Bronx Zoo, the curator phoned John Hunt to pick up another the next time he went to Africa. When the boa constrictor in the Ringling Circus made a slight tactical error and swallowed a valuable monkey, a message was sent to the private Hunt zoo on Long Island; if there was no such monkey in stock, would Hunt kindly get one on his next visit to Borneo? When that rare antelope called the bongo – so rare that it is worth nearly £1,000 – went down with the colic in the London Zoo, this radiogram reached John Hunt:

BONGO COLIC WHAT TREATMENT

He was supposed to know.

This was his fifth trip to South America, but it was the

first for his two sons, Hal and Roger. And yet they were not quite new to the animal game. Hal had hunted mountain lions in Colorado and Mexico, and both he and his younger brother had tended the collections in their father's Long Island supply zoo, where animals brought back from exploration trips were kept until they were bought by zoos, circuses or museums.

"Nobody knows," said John Hunt cautiously, "how many animals there are in the Amazon valley because so much of the country has not yet been explored. We're going to explore a new part of it on this trip, if all goes well. The Pastaza River."

"The Pastaza!" exclaimed Don Pedro. "That's known only as far as Andoas. Below that no white man has ever gone in and come out alive. Two tried last year. They were never heard of again. Why, the Indians down there are headhunters. Look up yonder. That's what they'll do to you."

He pointed to a strange object on the mantelpiece. It was a human head, but shrunken to the size of an orange.

Roger went over to get a close look at it. He hardly dared touch it.

"It must have been a baby's head."

"No, it was a man," said his father, "but the Jivaro Indians have a way of reducing them. You'll see when we get down there."

Roger looked doubtful. "But how about us?"

"I think we'll be in no danger. They do that to the heads of enemies, or the heads of relatives – and we're neither one."

The hotelman shook his head. "I wouldn't trust them as far as I could throw the cathedral," he said.

"What wouldn't the museums give to have specimens like that!" Hal exclaimed. "How about this one – would you sell it?"

The proprietor looked about nervously. Hal's father hastened to curb his son's enthusiasm.

"The police here would clap you in jail for making an offer like that," he said. "There's a law now against buying or selling heads. You can get imitations made out of goatskin or horsehide. But for the real article, you'll have to wait till we visit the Jivaros."

Roger was still uncomfortable.

"What do we want to go there for anyhow?" he asked. "I thought we were going down the Amazon."

"The Pastaza River is one of the headwaters of the Amazon. The Amazon doesn't start out by being the

Amazon, you know. It begins with a lot of little rivers flowing down from the snows of the Andes. The Pastaza is one of them. And a very interesting one because much of its course hasn't been charted."

"And because it goes through headhunter country," added Hal, amused to see his brother squirm. "We wouldn't want to miss that!"

Roger said nothing. He sauntered around behind Hal, quietly took hold of the crocodile's tail and, with a sudden jerk, landed his brother on the floor.

"Wait till I get you down in the Jivaro country," he said. "I'll help them do your head. Let's see, I think I'll have it fried and pickled. Only trouble is, no museum would want the ugly thing."

He got no further for Hal had grabbed him and was making a determined effort to insert him between the crocodile's jaws.

The hotel proprietor prudently removed the furniture from the vicinity of the struggling boys. He eyed their noisy antics with disapproval.

But John Hunt looked with some pride at his two sons. No man could want better pals on a jungle journey. Hal, finished with school and about to go to college, was as tall and strong as his father. Roger did not run to length, but he was alert and wiry, and brave enough, though he had admitted a natural uneasiness about associating with headhunters. Four years younger than his brother, he had jumped at the chance to spend his school holidays on an animal hunt. Their father had promised that if the boys made good on this adventure, their reward should be a trip to the South Seas.

A clerk handed John Hunt a cablegram. Hunt tore open the envelope and unfolded the message. The boys loosened their stranglehold upon each other and watched their father.

John Hunt read the cable. Then he read it again. As if not believing what he saw, he went over it a third time. The explorer's bronzed face did not grow pale, but there was a tenseness about the mouth and the fingers tightened on the paper. The boys impatiently waited.

"Well, Dad, tell us about it. What have you got there?"

Hunt laughed. "Somebody's trying to kid us," he said, and passed the cablegram to his sons. They read:

JOHN HUNT QUITO HOTEL QUITO ECUADOR THE AMAZON IS A BAD PLACE BETTER KEEP OUT OF IT

IF YOU WANT TO STAY HEALTHY AFFAIRS AT HOME WILL
REQUIRE YOUR ATTENTION

The cable was from New York. There was no signature.

2
The Following Shoes

"Who could have sent it?" wondered Hal.

"Perhaps one of the fellows up at the Explorers' Club trying to have a little fun with us," said Hunt, but his sons could see that he was not entirely satisfied with this explanation.

"Do you think there's any trouble at home?" Hal ventured.

"Of course not. If there were your mother would cable us."

Hal's forehead kinked the way it always did when he was puzzled.

"Looks to me as if we have a real mystery here," he said. "Now who could have a grudge against us? Who could want to stop us from going down the Amazon?"

"I don't know," his father said. "But I don't think we should pay too much attention to an anonymous message. If the fellow who sent this doesn't have the nerve to sign his name, perhaps he doesn't have the nerve to hurt us."

"Couldn't we trace it back? Doesn't anybody who sends

a cable have to give his name and address at the cable office?"

"Yes, but if he didn't want his identity known, he wouldn't give his real name and address."

Roger wasn't saying anything, but his eyes were growing larger every minute under the thrill of this strange situation. His father noticed the boy's excitement and said, "It's probably the work of some harmless crank. Suppose we just forget about it. We have to get up pretty early tomorrow morning so let's turn in. We get off at dawn — if that crazy flying Irishman has his plane ready."

"Perhaps I'd better drop round and see him right now," suggested Hal.

"Good idea. I'll go too," put in Roger.

"No," said his father, "you'd better get your beauty sleep."

Hal went out into the Plaza Independencia. A band concert was going on. The music echoed back from the great front of the cathedral and the archbishop's palace. The plaza was full of people, well-dressed citizens of Spanish blood, and Indians in flat hats and blanketlike ponchos.

What a city of beauty and mystery, thought Hal. It lay in a great bowl made by mountains, their snow-capped peaks gleaming in the moonlight. No wonder the people of Quito loved it. "From Quito to Heaven" they have always said.

As he slowed down, panting because of the 9,500-foot altitude, he reflected that this capital city of Ecuador was certainly next door to heaven. It was one of the highest capital cities in the world. But the air was not bitterly cold, for just outside of the city ran the equator. Still, it was chilly enough to make it hard to imagine that the equator was so near, and Hal buttoned his coat as he strolled out of the brightly lighted plaza into the dark, narrow streets of the old city.

It was necessary to walk with care over the rough cobblestones. The ancient adobe brick houses with their roofs of red tile covered with patches of green moss nearly closed overhead. It was like going through a tunnel.

Muffled shadows slid past in barefoot silence.

But Hal was conscious that one pair of feet somewhere behind him wore shoes. He thought nothing of it until, after he had turned right from Venezuela onto Sucre, he could still hear the shoes. He turned left on Pichincha. The shoes followed. Just for the fun of it, Hal went around the block. So did the owner of the shoes, always drawing closer. This was no longer very amusing. Hal quickened his pace.

He trod as lightly as possible, got well ahead, and then stepped into the intense shadow of the doorway of Terry O'Neill's house. He drew his flashlight from his pocket and waited.

Along came the persistent stranger. His footsteps were a bit uncertain now. He paused at one doorway after another and came at last to Hal's retreat.

Hal turned on the flashlight and threw the beam straight into the face of the man with shoes.

He was no Ecuadorean. He was too big and burly. Latin men are somewhat small and delicate, and the Indians are small and indelicate. This fellow could have passed as a prizefighter or a Chicago gangster. His face, twisted up by the sharp light, was inexpressibly cruel and sinister. His eyes gleamed like a surprised tiger's. No headhunter in the jungle could have looked more savage.

Hal could hardly refrain from beating on the door of his friend's house. He conquered this desire and said, "You were following me."

The man blinked. "Hey? You're crazy. I was just taking a walk."

"Funny you had to take the same walk that I did."

"What makes you think that?"

"I spotted you by your shoes."

"Shoes? Are you balmy? Lots of people in Quito wear shoes."

"Yes, but yours have a little tune of their own, and they went everywhere I did, even around the block." The stranger moved in threateningly, but Hal was a step above him and in a position to make things tough for him. A disturbance would bring out the whole neighbourhood.

The man's face broke into a sheepish grin.

"You're right, pal. I was following you. But I didn't mean nothing by it. I saw you were a Yank, and could speak my lingo, and I — well, I just wanted to ask the way to the Santo Domingo church. This being Sunday, I just thought I'd like to make a prayer and burn a few candles." And he raised his bloodshot eyes towards heaven.

"Straight down this street to the corner of Flores," said Hal.

"Thanks so much," said the stranger civilly enough, but as he turned out of the light there was a last flash of hate in his eyes that made Hal's spine creep. "I'll be seeing you."

"Don't make it too soon," was Hal's heartfelt reply and he turned to knock at Terry's door.

In the warm, comforting glow of Terry O'Neill's living room Hal related what had just happened in the street, and also the incident of the cablegram.

Terry was not the sort to take anything very seriously. He was a devil-may-care young aviator with a love for adventure that made him congratulate Hal on his success in finding some excitement.

"Looks as if you were going to have anything but a dull time," he said. "Do you suppose there is any connection between these two things? Have you an enemy in New York who might have sent an agent here to do you down?"

"We're rather short on enemies," said Hal. "Of course we have competitors. One very big competitor." He stopped suddenly and his forehead wrinkled. "I wonder—" he said. "Terry, perhaps you've given me an idea."

"Good. Do you still want to fly tomorrow morning?"

"Of course. How about the plane? Did you get those brakes fixed?"

"Well, not exactly," said Terry in his easy, Irish way. "But they'll probably do all right."

Lady Luck must play a pretty large part in Terry's affairs, Hal thought.

"Well," he said, "we'll be out at the field at dawn," and he rose to go.

"Do you want a bodyguard to escort you back to the hotel?"

"I'll make it," laughed Hal. But he did not go back as he had come. He took a roundabout route and walked in the middle of the street, eyes and ears alert. He got back to the hotel without incident and found his father and Roger asleep. He turned in, though he felt sure that he would lie awake all night, thinking. But it had been an active day. It takes plenty of rest to keep going in the thin air of sky-high Quito. In five minutes Hal, too, was asleep.

3
Dawn Flight

"All aboard for Green Hell!" cried Terry, revving up the motor of his tricky little four-seater Bonanza plane.

The Hunts climbed in with him. Their equipment and guns were stored in the baggage compartment. The Bonanza ambled bumpily down the grass airfield, gradually gaining speed.

When she was rolling at about seventy-five miles per hour a cross wind caught the ship and turned her directly towards a fire engine.

Terry could have angled her to one side or the other of the engine if his brakes had been good. They weren't. And without brakes, he couldn't stop. The airfield's crash sirens began to wail. The boys in the fire engine spilled out like popcorn.

But Terry, with a crazy Irishman's nerve, did the right thing, the desperate thing. He gave her the full gun. The plane roared across the field with the fire engine full ahead.

Would she rise enough to clear the great, red, metal monster that barred her path?

The nose wheel began to lift. The other two wheels bounded softly a few times, then rose. The plane was in the air. She cleared the fire engine by inches.

It's the people who know little about flying who don't realize its dangers. Hal and his father had both piloted planes but Roger was air green.

He looked up from the map he had been studying and, seeing the white faces of his brother and father, asked calmly, "Something wrong?"

Hal could have flayed him alive. And he could have administered a little flaying to the carefree pilot as well. Lady Luck must love this man!

The plane climbed a bit sluggishly. That was the fault not of the sturdy little Bonanza but of the altitude.

"What's your rate of climb?" asked Hal.

"About nine hundred feet a minute at sea level," Terry said. "But up here it's less than five hundred feet a minute."

"What's your service ceiling?" Hal was looking apprehensively at the towering, icy wall of mountains that they must cross before they could descend.

"This little tub," said Terry proudly, "will go up to seventeen thousand feet."

"But that will never get you over those peaks." Hal was looking at his map. Ecuador bristled with thirty tremendous volcanoes. Around Quito was a ring of giants. He looked out the window. There was Cotopaxi, the world's highest active volcano, cutting the sky at more than nineteen thousand feet. Cayambe and Antisana were almost as high.

"We'll slip through a pass," Terry assured Hal.

"But why are you going north now?"

"Just thought you'd like to have a look at the equator. And there it is. See that monument? It was put there in 1936 by a French survey mission to mark the exact equatorial line so that they could figure out the precise dimensions of this old planet. And now we're in the northern hemisphere." He banked the plane and sped back over the monument. At one instant they were in the northern hemisphere, at the next in the southern.

Roger was blowing on his chilled hands. "Pretty frosty equator," he commented.

"Is that road beneath us the Pan-American Highway?" asked John Hunt.

"Right," said Terry.

There it was, the wonder road that had now been practically completed all the way from Alaska to Patagonia.

"I'm going to make that trip sometime," vowed Roger.

"A good many people are making it right now," Terry said. "Yesterday I met a Scotsman who has a sheep ranch away down near Cape Horn. He had driven up all the way to Chicago, and was on his way back."

"But how about those breaks in the road?"

"There are three breaks in Central America. But you can put your car on a train or ship and get around them."

"The world's longest road," said John Hunt, looking down at the magic ribbon. "It will do a lot to tie the Americas together."

"But not so much as the aeroplane," said Terry, fondling the controls. For five years the flying Irishman had had his own plane. He had paid for it twice over by carrying passengers between Quito and Guayaquil on the coast, and Quito over the Andes to the jungle posts where rubber and quinine were gathered.

Hal wondered that he had never had an accident – and, as they raced towards the forbidding wall of rock and snow, hoped that he would not break his record now.

Presently the rampart ahead seemed to dissolve and a pass was visible. But what a pass! Great precipices frowned on either side of it. Couldn't the plane go higher and clear all this danger? Hal looked at the altimeter. It registered almost seventeen thousand feet. That meant that they were jammed up against the ceiling.

Suddenly even the ceiling failed them. The needle on the altimeter began to spin.

"Hey! That won't do," exclaimed Terry, trying to nose up the dropping plane.

They got out of the dangerous downdraught, but it left them only six hundred feet above the rocky bottom of the pass. In vain Terry tried to bring the plane up. So much banking and wheeling was necessary to avoid the cliffs that the little plane had no energy left for climbing. There was nothing to do but to follow all the twists and turns of the canyon and trust to luck that there would not be another downdraught. S turns and angles continually appeared ahead. Nobody was studying a map now. Roger's eyes popped as crag after crag rushed up to the windows and skimmed by with little to spare.

But a polo player would have been proud to manage his horse as Terry rode his plane. Hal thought of Ben Hur and his chariot race. Terry did not look like Ben Hur and he was not standing on a careering chariot but sitting quietly in the pilot's seat. But there was something of the heroic of all ages in the way he steered his irresistible motor around immovable objects. They melted away at his command. The impossible became possible.

Now, thank heaven, the floor of the canyon was falling a little. The savage walls were dropping back, beaten. With a final triumphant burst of speed the Bonanza swept out into a new world.

Gone were the arid, sandy wastes of the Pacific coast where rain almost never falls. Below stretched brilliant green forests that never lacked for water. Winding streams made silver alleys through the green.

"Look at the pink cloud," exclaimed Roger, hardly believing his own eyes.

Sure enough, a coloured cloud drifted over the forest.

"Butterflies," said Terry. "Just a few billion of them. And there's another cloud – parakeets. You get your clouds in all colours in this country – green, yellow, red, and mixed. Wait till you see the parrots and toucans. You'll think you're looking at a picture in technicolor."

"What's this stream beneath us?"

"That, my dear sir, is the Amazon. Or at least it's the Patate which becomes the Pastaza which becomes the Marañon which becomes the Amazon."

"And to think," said John Hunt, "that here within a hundred miles or so of the Pacific Ocean, the water turns its back on the Pacific and starts on a three-thousand-mile hike to the Atlantic."

"And we're starting on the same hike," said Hal. There was a thrill in that thought but a certain amount of fear too. The mystery of the unknown lay ahead. No other region on earth had so many secrets locked in its heart.

Presently the Patate joined hands with the Chambo to form the Pastaza, river of the Jivaro headhunters. A little frontier post called Topo passed beneath, then Mera, then Terry prepared to come down at the end of civilization, a jungle village called Puyo.

Hal was referring to his guidebook: "Here the known

world ends and the Amazonian wilderness begins. Penetration beyond Puyo is not possible even on horseback . . ."

It would have been possible by plane, but the plane was going back to Quito. The only other way was by boat. White men had never gone down the Pastaza, and on John Hunt's American Geographical Society map it was marked with a dotted line, meaning unexplored.

If this expedition were successful, that dotted line would be made solid. More than that, the animal life of a new region would be revealed. That was what most interested the three wild-animal collectors. A waterfall appeared below, a hanging bridge across the river, then a clearing. Terry was nosing down into it.

"What's your stalling speed?" asked Hal.

"Sixty-five."

It seemed a very small field to strike at a speed of more than a mile a minute. And no brakes!

At the far end of the field were a number of thatched huts. The plane plunged across the field, crushed the straw wall of a large hut, and came to a halt in the living-room-dining-room-bedroom among the members of a very startled household.

That was the introduction of the Hunts to the headhunters. Luckily none of the Indians was hurt, or four white heads might have been added speedily to the brown ones on the shelves.

4
Headhunters

Even so, for a moment it looked like rough going. The Indians snatched up spears and knives. Others came running into the hut and everyone was armed. The place resounded with the screams of women, the cries of children, and the menacing shouts of the warriors.

Then the smiling Irishman stuck his head out of the cockpit door. He called a merry greeting to an old man who turned out to be the chief. The angry chatter turned into a noisy welcome. These people knew Terry. This had been an outpost for the gatherers of cinchona, source of quinine, and Terry had been there many times.

Terry introduced his friends. The Indians conducted their guests in a triumphant procession through the village to the chief's house. The Hunts were astonished at the fine appearance of the village.

"Lucky we struck a straw hut instead of one of these," said Hal. Most of the houses in the village were well-built of solid timbers. One would never believe the place to be the home of savage headhunters. There were plots of corn, beans and bananas. Inside the houses could be seen looms on which cotton cloth was woven. On the shore of the swift Pastaza River were boats skilfully hollowed out of logs.

"They're really a very clever people," said Terry, noting the surprise of his guests. "And very brave. The Incas never conquered them. The Spaniards ruled them for only a short time – then the Indians rebelled and threw the Spaniards out. The government of Ecuador gets along with them by leaving them alone."

"Where do they get these shirts and shorts they are wearing?" asked Hal.

"They make them. But when they go to war they strip off their clothes and paint their bodies in bright colours."

Even in shirts and shorts, some of the men looked a bit wild. "They need haircuts," remarked Roger. Their hair was black, long and flowing, and decorated with toucan feathers.

"In every Jivaro there are two persons," said Terry, "one civilized and the other a savage. And you never know which one you are going to meet. That's what makes them interesting."

In the chief's house, the walls of which were hung with blowguns, spears, bows and arrows, and the skins of magnificent *tigres* and panthers, they were served a strange lunch.

"I never saw such large eggs," said Roger. "The chickens here must be giants."

"The chicken that laid those eggs," Terry told him, "was ten feet long and had teeth like a sausage grinder. You're eating alligator's eggs. How do you like them?"

Roger made a wry face. "I liked them until you told me that."

"And what's this steak?" asked Hal. "Surely they don't have cattle down here."

"That's from the tail of an iguana. It's an enormous lizard, five or six feet long, that is plentiful in these woods. You'll probably want one of them for your collection. And that other meat that tastes like veal – it's a slice of mountain lion. But never mind, you'll eat stranger things than these before you get done with the Amazon."

"You're right," said John Hunt, who knew from former trips to the lower river what experiences the boys were in for. He ate heartily, but the boys were very easily satisfied. It would take them a little time to get used to Amazonian cookery. Their appetites were not improved by a glance at a grim row of heads on a high shelf. One head was perched alone over the door.

"That one seems to have the place of honour," said John Hunt.

The old chief did not understand the English words but he saw that his guest was talking about the head over the door. He spoke to Terry and Terry translated.

"He says that's his grandfather. You see, this preservation of heads isn't quite as barbarous as most people suppose. Didn't the Egyptians keep not only the heads but the entire bodies of their kings mummified so that they would last? This is more or less the same idea. The chief says he was very fond of his grandfather and wants to keep him nearby always. It's the Jivaro way of showing respect."

Hal objected, "That's all right for friends and relatives, but why do they preserve the heads of enemies? Surely that's not to show respect."

"Yes it is," Terry insisted. "They believe that by keeping the head of a strong man they get his strength. They don't bother to shrink the heads of weaklings – it's a long, hard job and they don't consider it worth while."

"Unless they are making them for sale as curiosities to tourists," put in John Hunt.

"Yes. But if they are making them to keep in their own huts, they preserve only the heads of fine warriors."

"Then we ought to feel honoured if they decide to tan and pickle us," said Roger.

"That's right," laughed Terry. "And I may as well warn you that they believe there's some special magic in white heads. They think that the white man is especially wise and powerful and that anyone who gets his head will be wise and powerful too."

Roger made a mock show of holding his head tightly to his shoulders.

"Don't worry," said Hal. "They won't mistake your bean for something wise and powerful."

"Oh, is that so?" fumed Roger. "I bet they'll take mine first."

"Have it that way if you prefer," said Hal.

"I wonder if the chief would explain how they shrink these heads," John Hunt suggested. "It must be quite an art."

Terry passed on the question to the chief, who nodded gravely and began to explain, Terry translating.

"Everything must be done according to ceremony," said the chief, "otherwise the virtue of the hero is lost. The medicine man performs certain religious rites. That is to comfort the spirit of the dead man so that it will not be disturbed by what follows. We sew the lips together so that the spirit may not escape. Then we make a slit in the back of the scalp and take out the skull. Of course we could not shrink the head if the skull remained in it. The shrinking is done by filling the head with hot sand. When it cools it is taken out and more hot sand put in. Night and day for three days — sometimes for a week if we wish the head to be very small. That is all. It is simple."

"He is modest," smiled John Hunt. "But the truth is that no other tribes on earth have been able to do it as well. A good many have tried it."

"And it's a lot more complicated than he says," Terry added. "There's a tanning process in a secret liquid made of herbs and spices, and a boiling process, and smoking, and night and day all during the hot-sand process the face must be stroked with a smooth stone. They model it just as a sculptor would model clay or wax. It takes a real artist to do it so as to keep the natural appearance of the features."

John Hunt was examining the heads on the shelf. "The American Museum of Natural History wants one for its anthropology collection. Will you ask him if we may buy one?"

At first the chief shook his head. But Terry was eloquent. He explained about the museum. It was one of the greatest in the world. Thousands of people came to it daily. When they saw this exhibit they would respect the skill of the Jivaros. Was there not some great hero he would like to honour? There was no better way he could honour him than by placing him in this great museum.

The chief looked up at his grandfather. But no, he could not part with him. He took down another fine head.

"This was one of our noblest warriors, and a wise and good man. He will go to your country."

"What was his name?"

The chief gave a name that sounded something like Charlie. And so on all the rest of their journey the Hunts' silent little travelling companion was called Charlie.

Terry negotiated. The chief fixed the price at twenty-five dollars. John Hunt paid fifty dollars.

"Why pay him more than he asks?" said Terry.

"It's only fair. After all, the museum will pay several hundred dollars for this specimen."

And so Charlie was launched on his adventures.

"And now will you tell him of our plan to go down the Pastaza?" Terry did so, but the chief protested strongly.

Terry looked serious. "You'd better give up this scheme. He says you'd be killed. He and his people are friendly.

But he can't speak for the people down river. They are very savage and they have never made peace with the white man."

But Hunt was not to be swerved from his purpose. "They have no guns," he said.

"No, but they have blowpipes with poison darts, and spears and poison-tipped arrows. And they know how to use them."

"Yes, but I'm hoping we can make friends with them."

"Perhaps they'll shoot before you can make friends."

"We'll have to take that chance. It's important. I've promised the American Geographical that I'd make a try at exploring the lower Pastaza. And there's the chance that we'll come upon some new varieties of animals. Ask the chief if he can supply us with a boat."

The chief gloomily agreed. But he insisted that his guests should stay with him overnight.

"Where would we sleep?" asked Hal.

"On those wooden platforms."

"They look a bit hard."

"You'll be too tired to notice."

Roger was not too keen about staying. "More alligator's eggs," he moaned.

"Boys," their father said, "you wanted to come on this

trip. If you've changed your minds you can fly back with Terry."

The words had effect. The very idea of giving up their great adventure reconciled the boys to platform beds and alligator's eggs.

But there were no alligator's eggs for supper. Instead there was a very delicious slab of tender white meat that tasted a little like fish and a little like chicken. Roger ate it with great relish and never thought to ask what it was until he had finished.

The chief explained that it was a slice of a large boa constrictor that had recently invaded the village. Roger turned green. "You mean they eat snakes?"

"Why not?" said Terry. "Wasn't it good?"

"Yes, but nobody eats snakes."

His father smiled. "By 'nobody' I suppose you mean none of your neighbours on Long Island. But you're going to learn that other people have other ways, and they are often quite as good as ours. If Frenchmen can eat snails, and Chinese can eat birds' nests, and Japanese can eat seaweed, and hill tribes in India can eat grasshoppers, and Long Islanders can eat slimy living oysters, why shouldn't the Amazon people eat the foods that nature has provided for them?"

"I know," said Roger, determined to show as much stamina as his father. "If you can eat it, I can. Pass the snake, please."

He helped himself to another generous slice and manfully ate it. "Good stuff!" he said, smacking his lips. But he was still a little green around the gills.

That night, tossing on his wooden bed, he dreamed that he had turned into a boa constrictor and a human giant was swallowing him. He thrashed his tail vigorously, but the giant got him all down and then smacked his lips and said, "Snakes are very good to eat."

Terry had flown back to Quito in the afternoon. They were sorry to see him go. He and his plane seemed like the last links with civilization. Hal woke towards dawn and lay listening to the unearthly howls, screams, and coughs that rose from the surrounding forest. Yes, they had come to the right place for animals! He was glad that they were sleeping inside four walls. But how about tomorrow night, and many nights to come?

But Hal did not think much about the dangers that lay ahead – he had camped in the wilds before. His thoughts went back to a face in Quito, a face illuminated in the glow of his flashlight and now stamped upon his memory.

But why worry? They had left that face far behind. The
following shoes could hardly follow into the Amazonian
jungle. Or could they?

5
The Condor's Shadow

At dawn he was out at the river's edge, loading the boat. It was an Indian-made canoe, hollowed out of a single log. Hal reckoned the length of it to be about twenty feet, and its beam was a little better than two feet. It was just the right size for three or four men and their kit.

The interior of the log had been chipped and burned out with great skill so that all that was left was a shell about an inch thick. Hal admired the Indians' handiwork. It must have taken pretty nice judgement to make that wall just thick enough and not to cut through it at any point.

The boat would slide over the water like rain over a duck's back. The only trouble was that it would slide sidewise as well as lengthwise, for it had no keel. Of course it would clear the bottom more easily without a keel.

"But we'll have to part our hair in the middle," Hal reflected. The utmost care would be necessary to keep the craft from rolling over.

The first job was to pack the kit evenly, distributing its weight so that the balance would be perfect. Working room must be left for the paddlers. The surface of the baggage must be flat so that it would be easy to crawl or jump over it in case it was necessary to change places. Guns must be where they could be reached quickly. But both the guns and other objects too heavy to float must be secured under a thwart or tied so that they would not sink in the event of an upset.

Hal went to work. When the others came out he had everything stowed to his own satisfaction.

His father looked over the job critically.

"You haven't forgotten Canada," was his way of commending Hal. They had canoed together on many northern rivers. But Roger was without experience. This would be his initiation into river travel.

Hal and his father went back to the house but had no sooner reached it than they were startled by a yell from the river. They looked back to see the newly packed boat already upside down in the middle of the stream and Roger's head bobbing beside it. They were not worried about Roger. He could swim. But the boat was being carried swiftly downstream. Soon it would be in the rapids, and farther down were falls.

They ran to the river and plunged in. In this swift current there were not likely to be crocodiles, stingrays, or anacondas. They joined Roger, who was already manfully trying to push the boat towards shore. In a few moments they had it beached. Roger crawled up onto the bank, dripping and crestfallen.

"I just wanted to try her out."

Hunt eyed his younger son with disapproval but could not help grinning at his sorry appearance.

"Your middle name is Mischief," he remarked.

"Everything stayed in the boat," Hal said, inspecting his packing. Most of the bundles were fairly waterproof, but all the kit was put out on the bank to dry in the hot sun and was then repacked.

Roger was very quiet for a while but as his clothes dried out his spirits revived.

"We're off!" he whooped an hour later as they left the shore. The chief and his warriors stood on the bank making gestures of farewell. One of their number was in the boat. He would accompany the explorers to the edge of hostile country. More than that he would not promise. But John Hunt hoped that he could be persuaded to go on down the unknown part of the Pastaza, the river of the dotted line.

There was nothing to suggest any danger ahead. The sun shone gloriously, the monkeys chattered in the treetops, parrots and macaws made waves of brilliant colour, and far off to the west over the green forest loomed the snowy head of twenty-thousand-foot Chimborazo, looking down towards the Pacific on one side and, on the other side, to the travellers on their way to the Atlantic.

A bend in the stream, and the friendly Jivaro village disappeared. Dense jungle closed in on both sides. The river was about a hundred feet wide. The water was glassy smooth but was hurrying forward as if eager to get to an appointment. The four paddles had little to do except to keep the boat straight.

"Look at the birds," cried Hal.

Roger looked up.

"No, look down. Down in the water."

Sure enough, at the bottom of the clear, shallow stream small dark birds were fluttering about, seeking food.

There was no time to watch them, for the boat sped on.

"Water ouzels," Hunt said.

"But they were flying under water."

"You might call it flying. They beat their wings to help them move through the water. They're hunting for snails and water insects. They can stay down two or three minutes."

A shadow as of a small black cloud seemed to pass over the water. They looked up to see a wonder above as great as the wonder they had just seen below.

"A condor," exclaimed Hunt. It easily measured ten feet from tip to tip.

The Indian was much excited. "Very bad," he said out of his little store of English acquired from serving American cinchona men. He made passes over his head as if to put a protective charm over himself.

"The Indians are very superstitious about the condor," Hunt said. "I'm afraid he thinks it's a bad omen for our trip. You see, the condor hangs around where anything is dead, or where he thinks something is going to be."

"Here he comes back. We'll see who's dead." And Roger grabbed his .22.

"Save your ammunition. The bird isn't doing any harm and it's no good to eat. Besides, you couldn't hurt it with that popgun."

"He's immense," murmured Hal as the bird made another circle.

"The world's largest flying bird," said Hunt. "And although it is so heavy, it can fly higher than any other bird. It can get along without eating for forty days if necessary, but when a condor does get a chance to eat, he can put away eighteen pounds of meat at a sitting."

"I know," Roger said. "They carry away lambs and babies."

"Not exactly. They're not afraid to attack anything large, even a horse, if he looks weak or sick. But they never fly away with their food. Their talons are too weak to lift a heavy load."

The condor sailed away, discouraged, but he left behind him a very much disturbed Indian.

"No good, no good," he insisted, backwatering vigorously with his paddle. "We go back, we go back."

But it was impossible to go back at the moment, for a powerful current had seized the boat, making argument quite unnecessary.

From around the bend came the hollow roar of rapids. Whirling, boiling eddies burst up around the boat, as if sticks of dynamite were being set off at the bottom of the stream. Choppy waves began to bob up.

They swept around the curve, and the full roar of angry waters struck their ears. Ahead, the river was full of dancing white figures. Sharp rocks sent fountains of spray into the air. Over rounded rocks the water rolled in big humps.

Napo, the Indian, was in the bow, John Hunt in the

stern. Napo pointed to a chute between two big rocks. All the paddles joined forces to speed the boat like an arrow through the narrow passage. The faster the better. In water like this it was necessary to have plenty of steerage way. The boat must go faster than the current if it was to be successfully steered around rocks.

The water humped itself into a ridge as it shot through between the rocks. The canoe rode the hump like a cowboy on horseback. The spray thrown up by the rocks soused everybody on board.

No one noticed the wetting. The paddles were going like mad. The boat rolled and darted, dodged and plunged. A rollercoaster was tame compared with this.

Roger let out a whoop and the others joined him, regardless of age. This was the sort of thing that would make boys out of greybeards. The blood coursed swiftly and the spine tingled. Rocks fled past.

The boat plunged into a hollow and Napo disappeared. The bow seemed to be pointed straight towards the bottom. John Hunt and Hal backwatered powerfully to bring the bow up, and there was Napo no worse for wear. But his next yell had a watery gurgle in it.

The dugout was performing acrobatic feats. It seemed miraculous that a boat cut out of a single log could be so nimble. It almost seemed to snake through between rocks or to draw in its stomach when it went over them. Like its passengers, it would shout with joy if it could.

Now it shot downhill in a last victorious sweep and then ran out under its own momentum, paddles idle, into a smooth, broad basin.

It was pleasant to relax and to look back at the boiling staircase down which they had come.

"There's a lot of that sort of thing in these Amazon rivers," Hunt said. "I suppose you know the origin of the word Amazon?"

"Doesn't it have something to do with a tribe of warrior women that the first explorers discovered?" Hal said.

"That's one theory. The other is that the river is named after the Indian word Amassona, meaning boat destroyer. It's not just the rapids that make it deserve this name. Some of the rivers are full of dangerous logs floating just below the surface. And where the main stream of the Amazon becomes as wide as a sea there are pretty bad storms. And then there's the bore."

"What's a bore?" asked Roger.

"A moving wall of water something like a tidal wave. It rushes up the river from the ocean. It may be ten or twelve feet high."

"I'd like to see that," Roger said.

His father smiled grimly. "You will. But I hope we're in a bigger boat than this when it comes."

"How soon do we get a boat big enough so we can collect some animals?"

"As soon as we get out of this river. Nothing bigger than this would get us down the Pastaza. But we don't need to wait to collect little animals — and sometimes they're just as important as the big ones."

A sullen roar ahead warned that collecting would have to be postponed a little while longer. This roar was not like the last. It was a deeper thunder. The source of the thunder could not be seen. The river simply dropped out of sight, and where it disappeared vapour rose into the air.

"Falls!" exclaimed Hal. "We'd better stop and look this one over."

At the right was a little bay in which an eddy circled. They pulled in to the shore, beached the boat, and then picked their way through the jungle to the river's edge where they could inspect the falls.

At one point the water made a sheer drop of twelve feet into a mass of jagged rocks.

"That's where we *don't* want to go," remarked John

Hunt. "But see that slide over yonder? We can't shoot it, but perhaps we could ease the boat down by the painter."

This project proved fully as exciting as shooting the rapids. The boat was paddled to a position near the head of the chute but close to the shore where the current was not too strong. Everybody was tense with anticipation. Napo seemed to have forgotten the shadow of the condor.

They stepped out into the swift but shallow stream. The water came about chest high. What a good way to escape the tropical sun! The hunters did not wear the heavy hunting clothes common in northern climes. Thin shirt and thin trousers and a pair of South American sandals called *alpargatas* completed their costume. There was nothing that could be spoiled by a wetting – unless you were to count the tobacco in John Hunt's pipe.

The contents of the canoe were fairly well protected. Even the guns were in waterproof cases. Ammunition was packed in an aluminium box as waterproof as a bottle, and camera, films, medicines, and valuable papers in another.

But Charlie, the Jivaro head, was merely tied by his hair to a thwart. He had weathered sun, rain and wave while alive and was just as capable of doing so now.

Hal and Napo held the painter. This rope attached to the bow of the boat was made of plaited vines and was as strong as hemp. They braced themselves against the rocks and let the painter out a few inches at a time, letting the boat into the chutes stern first.

Roger and his father hung onto the stern, one on each side. It was their job to guide the canoe down through the rocks.

"If the water sweeps you off your feet, Roger, hang onto the gunwale."

The boat was in a slide of water that slanted down like the roof of a house. The bottom was very uneven. Now Roger would be perched on a rock where the water was only ankle deep, and then he would drop into a hole up to his neck. He grimly hung onto the gunwale. The boat helped him as much as he helped the boat.

"Not too fast," John Hunt yelled to the two who were paying out the painter. He could hardly make himself heard above the roar.

He spoke just too late. The advancing stern pushed him from his slippery foothold and he went over like a ninepin into a foaming whirlpool.

This could be serious. Whirled around beneath the surface, he might easily be badly bruised against the rocks. He might be knocked unconscious and be unable to come up.

The three looked anxiously for some sign of him. When they were about to abandon the boat to its fate and go to the rescue, his head emerged from under the stern. It came up slowly and Hal laughed with relief when he saw that his father's pipe was still stuck in his teeth. The dripping face wore a surprised and rather offended expression. Dad was not used to being man-handled in this fashion by the forces of nature.

A little later it was Dad who laughed. They were all aboard once more and slipping down a fast but not dangerous stretch under some overhanging trees. Hal was bent over, groping for something in the bottom of the boat. A dead snag on one of the branches slipped under his belt, and before he could make any remark on the situation, he was suspended in air and the boat was going on without him. He tried to grab the boat but got only a sack of potatoes.

There he was left, in a very undignified position, tail up and head down, hanging grimly to a bag of spuds. The snag broke and he and his potatoes took a bath.

The canoe had been beached on a sand spit and Hal was greeted hilariously as he staggered out, still holding his burden.

Lunch was served on the sand spit. During the afternoon

there were more rapids, and more, and more, until it was a very weary foursome who beached the canoe late in the afternoon on a bank under some large trees that would serve as a hotel for the night.

6
The Face on the Trail

It seemed an ideal place to make camp. A lovely pool a hundred yards across lay before it. Fish punctuated its smooth surface with darts and circles. Beyond the pool the jungle wall rose black but was topped by flowering trees that glowed yellow and crimson in the setting sun. Lazy white egrets drifted past.

Under the great ceibas where they proposed to make camp there was no undergrowth near the river bank, but it began a few yards back.

Where the clear space ended and the jungle began, John Hunt found a slight opening.

"Looks like a trail," he said, and he turned to Napo. "Indians?"

Napo looked doubtful. Then he examined the soft ground and pointed to footprints. But they were not made by human feet.

"Look, boys," Hunt said. "Here's your introduction to the animals of the Amazon. These stabs are made by the hooves of peccaries."

"Aren't they wild boars?" said Hal. "I was reading up about them. It seems that they go around in gangs and don't hesitate to attack men."

"You're right. When they come around, the safest place is up a tree. I knew one explorer who was treed for three days and three nights." He examined other tracks. "Looks to me as if the animals come down here to drink at night. These tracks were made by a capybara," pointing to tracks made by queerly splayed feet. "It's the world's biggest rat – as big as a sheep. And these are deer tracks."

"Yes," said Hal. "I'd recognize them anywhere," remembering the deer trails of Colorado, Canada, and the Maine woods.

"But there is something I never saw before."

The tracks he indicated were smooth and round as if they had been made by large saucers.

"*Tigre!*" exclaimed Napo. "This place no good."

"That's the *tigre* all right," Hunt admitted.

"What's a tee-gray?" Roger wanted to know, for that was how both his father and Napo had pronounced the word.

"It's the Spanish word for tiger. All through Mexico and South America they call this animal the *tigre* although it is not really a tiger. It wears spots, not stripes. When we get over the Brazilian border where Portuguese is spoken we'll hear it called the *onca*, meaning ounce. Our own name for it is jaguar. But call it what you like, it's the king of the forest."

"No good," wailed Napo. "We go back."

"He's got the we-go-backs again," Hal said in disgust. "What a chance to get some photographs tonight if they come down to drink!"

"And what a chance for them to get some nice little explorers," wondered Roger.

"Don't worry," Dad said. "They're not likely to attack us if we leave them alone. Besides, we'll be well up out of their way – in our hammocks."

The method of camp making was new to Hal and

Roger, accustomed to the tents, canvas flies and sleeping bags of the north. The jungle traveller cannot be burdened with heavy gear. He sleeps in the open. For him, no canvas house completely sealed in with canvas door and mosquito netting over the windows. The Minneapolis clerk who takes a run up into the Minnesota lake country for a few nights carries more elaborate gear for camping in this land where the most dangerous beast is the mosquito than the experienced explorer takes for a year's trek through the Amazon jungle.

In ten minutes camp was set up. It consisted merely of three hammocks strung between the trees.

The hammock is the bed of Amazonia. It was invented by the Amazon Indians and we owe our garden hammocks to their invention. Even in the town, the hammock is the only bed in most homes. All that one sees in the daytime is iron hooks in the wall – but at night the hammocks are strung up and the living room becomes a bedroom. Hotels, too, are furnished only with hooks in the wall. The guest is supposed to bring his own hammock.

But there are a few tribes in hammockland who do not subscribe to the custom, and the Jivaros are one of them. So Napo, instead of stringing up a hammock, made a hole in the ground. He was going to bury himself. The earth, superheated during the day, keeps the body warm during the night, which is sometimes surprisingly chilly.

After the beds, three aerial and one subterranean, had been made, Napo took up his bow and arrows. "Me get fish," he said.

Dad suggested that Roger would probably like to see how fishing was done with bow and arrows. Roger went along, but he seemed to have something else on his mind. He kept glancing back at the break in the jungle where animals came out at night, and where Indians, too, might emerge. Who could tell? Anybody watching him would have seen that he was up to no good. But nobody was watching.

He went with Napo along the river bank and stayed with him until Napo had spotted a trout swimming about a foot beneath the surface and had pierced him with an arrow. Napo took the fish back to camp to be baked in mud for supper – but Roger went to the boat, got something from it, and disappeared into the jungle. Presently he strolled back into camp and joined in building the fire.

It was now quite dark under the trees but a flickering yellow light began to radiate from the fire. Ghostly shadows leaped about. A scream or two came from the jungle as a preliminary to the nightly chorus.

Hal shivered slightly and glanced at the point where the trail entered the undergrowth. Then his eyes froze.

"Dad, look," he whispered. "An Indian."

His father looked. There was no doubt about it. An Indian face peered from the brush. The light was too poor to see it distinctly.

"Must be Napo," Hunt said. "He's getting wood."

"Yes, but he's getting it down near the river."

Napo came up the bank with a load of driftwood.

Hal reached for his gun but his father said, "Don't be hasty, they may be friendly. Let's try a present first." And he took a small mirror out of his pocket. Indians liked mirrors.

Napo, following the gaze of the others, was much puzzled at what he saw. In his astonishment he dropped his load of wood on his own toes. This brought a yell out of him that further startled Hal and his father, but did not seem to disturb the face on the trail. And Hal noticed that Roger, too, was strangely calm.

That kid has more nerve than I gave him credit for, he thought.

"Can't see him plainly," Dad complained, blinking. "But he looks pretty small. He may be just a boy. Perhaps only curious. Anyhow I'll try him with this present."

"But I'll back you up with the gun if there's any monkey business," Hal promised.

Dad walked forward gingerly. Hal held his gun and his breath. Roger made a sound something like a snicker, but it may have been just a gasp of terror. The face on the trail did not move.

Dad was within a few feet of it now. He stopped and began to laugh. Then he reached into the brush and pulled out the head. It was Charlie.

Roger exploded with merriment and rolled on the ground, kicking and roaring. Hal laid down his gun, took Roger up by the seat of his shorts, and started towards the river. Roger wriggled free and disappeared into the brush. He continued laughing like a hyena.

Hal began to laugh too, and only Napo remained serious, looking from one to another of his strange companions as if doubting their sanity. Then he gave up trying to understand them and went to take the fish out of the fire.

He took out a mud ball baked hard and dry, broke it on a stone, and there was the fish, cooked to a turn. With some potatoes baked in the same fire it made an appetizing meal.

Then the Hunts retreated into their hammocks, and

Napo into his hole. The blankets in the hammocks would be appreciated before morning. As for the mosquito nets, especially made with sleeves to fit over the hammock strings, they were not used for there seemed to be no mosquitoes around this camp site. To discourage ants and other small pests from crawling out from the trees into the hammocks, the hammock strings had been creosoted.

Roger squirmed and twisted, for he had never before tried sleeping in a hammock.

"Don't lie straight along it," his father advised him. "Lie on the diagonal. Then you won't be so likely to fall out."

But Roger was not one who could learn very much from being told. He had to learn from bitter experience.

Soon he and his father were sleeping soundly. Hal, clutching camera and flash bulbs, tried to keep awake but presently joined the others in slumberland.

Napo had buried himself well aside from the animal trail. His head projected oddly from the ground and moved this way and that as he looked about in the light of the dying fire, but before long it dropped and his eyes closed.

And, as the four slept, the forest awoke. "Awake for it is night," the animals seemed to say.

The cicadas began with a piercing chirp but managed to develop it into a screeching whistle. The tree frogs drummed, hoo-hooed, and croaked. The nightjar made a sound like the wail of a dying ghost, if ghosts ever die. Strange creatures that had not yet been given long Latin names by the zoologists added their contribution to the din.

Then there was a deep grumbling cough. Instantly all other noise was hushed. That was the honour accorded to the *tigre*, king of the forest.

7
Jungle Night

An ear-splitting yell broke the silence.

Dad woke with a start and turned on his flashlight. Again that wild yell. It seemed to be Roger's voice.

Both Dad and Hal beamed their lights on the trail. They fully expected to see Roger in the jaws of a *tigre*. But there was no sign of either animal or boy.

"Help! Help!" screeched Roger's voice. The lights swept around and focused on him.

He had gone stark, staring mad. He was doing a combination of the samba and the Highland fling, and splitting the welkin with his cries. He clawed himself furiously, tearing off his shirt and trousers and, quite naked, continued to leap and prance, slapping and grabbing at different parts of his anatomy.

"Hey, can't you do something?" he wailed.

John Hunt climbed out of his hammock, chuckling.

"I think you've found just the right thing to do," he said. "Dance boy, dance!"

He played his light along the ground.

"There they go. Get out of their line of march."

A black band was moving across the ground. It was about a foot wide. The procession seemed to have no end in either direction.

"What are they?" asked Hal.

"Army ants. Sometimes they make a procession a mile long. They eat everything that comes in their way – boys included. See the officers."

Along the edges of the column were ants that did not march steadily forward with the others, but kept running back and forth as if to keep the privates in line.

He went to the fireplace and got a stick that still glowed at one end.

"All right, Roger. Here comes the doctor. But I hope you won't think that the remedy is worse than the disease."

With difficulty Roger stood still as his father went over him, applying the hot coal to the rear ends of ants which had sunk their enormous pincers into his flesh. The ants thus attacked from behind relaxed their hold and dropped off.

Roger's wild antics had already broken off many of the bodies, leaving the heads and jaws firmly transfixed in the flesh. More drastic means had to be used to dislodge these. They must be picked out with the point of a knife. Then the wounds were spotted with merthiolate until Roger looked like a pink-and-white leopard, or perhaps an Indian in his war paint.

"But how did they get at you in the hammock?" his father asked.

Roger was sheepish. "Well, I wasn't in the hammock. I fell out. I was too sleepy to get back in, and anyhow the ground felt better than the old hammock. But I can't understand why they didn't go after Napo."

They hadn't thought of Napo. They played their lights on the spot where he should have been. There was a little mound of fresh earth and the ants streamed over it. The experienced Napo had gone completely underground.

Roger fingered his wounds. "How those fellows can bite!"

"Did you know that the Indians use an ant of that sort to stitch wounds? They make the ant bite the edges of the wound together. Then they cut off the ant's body. The jaws stay locked and keep the wound closed until it heals."

"An Indian village must have a merry time of it when one of these armies bears down upon it," Hal speculated.

"The best thing to do is to move out and leave the village to the ants. The Indians stay at a safe distance in the jungle until the army has passed. The ones whose houses were on the line of march are lucky. Their places are cleaned of vermin and insects."

The tail of the procession went by. Napo seemed to know when this happened and his head cautiously emerged from the ground. Roger, however, had had enough of Mother Earth – he put on his clothes, wrapped himself in his blanket, and climbed back into the hammock.

Again, darkness and silence. The forest, disturbed by the commotion in the camp, kept the peace for a while. Then one sound after another invaded the stillness until the boiler factory was going full blast once more.

Hal lay awake now, hoping that some of the denizens of the woods might get thirsty. But they had evidently been thrown off their routine by the strange doings in their forest. Only the most dull-witted of them would come tonight.

At last he arrived – the big half-wit of the woods. Hal heard a crackling of the underbrush as if some very heavy animal were approaching. He waited until he felt sure that it had left the brush and was crossing the camp site. Then he turned on his flash. The animal stopped and stood peering into the light. Hal's flash bulb flared, and he had a photograph of a tapir.

A good animal photographer takes his picture first and

then makes observations. If he should make his observations first the animal might be gone before the photograph could be taken. With the tapir safely tucked away in his camera, Hal proceeded to study the beast.

It was the first of its kind that he had ever seen, but he knew it from the pictures in the many natural-history books that he had studied. And yet, he could not help being astonished by the real thing.

Here was the largest wild animal in South America. This specimen must weigh twenty stone. It was some five feet high and six feet long. It seemed to have been put together with spare parts of other animals. It had the body of a huge pig, the mane of a horse and the trunk of an elephant.

Hal knew that some scientists contend that this is the elephant's American cousin. The beast's trunk was very short but it was evidently used in exactly the same way as the trunk of an elephant, to gather food and tuck it into the mouth beneath.

Fascinated by the light, the horse-pig-elephant stood quite still. The Cincinnati Zoo wanted just such a specimen. Hal was helpless. Even if they could catch the animal they could not transport it in a treacherous canoe down a boiling river. If only these beasts came in smaller, more portable editions.

As if in answer to his prayer, there was a rustling in the brush and out came the pocket edition. Well, it would not exactly fit into a pocket but it might be accommodated even in a crowded canoe.

It was a baby tapir, not a dull brown colour like its mother, but gaily marked with yellow stripes and white spots. It made a whimpering noise as it waddled to its mother and proceeded to help itself to some liquid refreshment.

Hal was about to prod his father awake with the butt end of his rifle when it occurred to him that it would be a great feather in his cap if he could capture this little specimen singlehanded. After all, it shouldn't be much of a problem. Surely the mother would not make too much trouble.

He tried to remember what he had read about the tapir – some authority had said that it was a very mild-mannered beast. And it was extremely nearsighted. Perhaps he could get almost up to it without its realizing what was going on.

He slid softly out of his hammock and crept forward, still keeping his light shining full into the tapir's weak eyes.

He tried to calculate his chances. If he frightened the tapir, which way would it probably run? He knew that tapirs habitually take refuge in rivers. Probably this animal, if alarmed, would make straight for the water. The little fellow could not move so fast and might be easily captured.

But the best-laid plans of mice and men and boy naturalists gang aft agley. A twig cracked underfoot. The tapir started, but not towards the river. Lowering its head, it plunged straight into the light. Hal was about to learn that even a mild-mannered mamma will defend its young.

The charging tapir gave voice, but it did not make the thunderous roar that one might expect from an animal of its size. It screamed like a mad horse, the scream ending in a shrill whistle.

The other campers awoke with a start. Dad and Roger tumbled out of their hammocks and Napo rooted up out of his burrow like a hedgehog at the first call of spring.

None of the them had time to act before the three-hundred-pound battery reached Hal.

Hal had the presence of mind to leap for a branch in order to let the brown torpedo pass beneath him – but the branch broke and he landed squarely on the tapir's back. Something else that he had read flashed painfully into his mind. The jaguar attacks the tapir by leaping onto its back; but the supposedly stupid tapir knows enough to tear its way through thorny underbrush or under half-fallen logs or low branches by which the jaguar is crushed and brushed off, a bleeding, mangled mass of pulp.

Horrified by this thought, Hal lost no time in tumbling from his mount. He breathed a sigh of relief as he lay on the quiet earth. But if he had thought that the tapir was done with him, he was mistaken. Even without the light, it knew where its enemy lay. A tapir's eyes may be poor, but its senses of smell and hearing are acute.

Hal heard it coming like an express train, its whistle wailing. He struggled to his knees and threw himself out of the way. As the lumbering beast hurtled past, two flashlights suddenly spotted it and then there was the roar of a gun.

Even the thick-hided combination of horse, boar and elephant with a touch of rhinoceros could not resist a 130-grain expanding bullet from Dad's .270 Winchester. The tapir turned a heavy somersault and lay still.

Hal hurried to the scene. He must find the youngster. That was not hard. The baby was already running to its mother. Reaching her, it settled down and began to take its last drink.

Hal had a tinge of regret. His companions looked on and nobody had anything to say for a moment. They let the little fellow drink his fill.

Hal stooped to stroke the smooth, colourful skin of the little orphan.

"Never mind," he said. "We'll make it up to you. We'll take you to a nice zoo where you can have the best of food and a swimming pool all to yourself. And no *tigres* to bother you. That's a promise."

8
Down the Dotted Line

Next morning there were more rapids, and then a great fall. They had to portage around it, first carrying the gear, and then the canoe. When the canoe was repacked at the base of the fall they all stepped aboard again – all except Napo.

He stood on the shore and looked stubborn.

"Me go back," he said.

Dad argued with him, but it was no use. This fall marked the end of the country that he knew. Beyond was the unknown, filled with mysterious terrors. He did not know the people. His only comment upon them was that they were very bad.

He would walk back home by a trail bordering the river. It would take him about two days to make his village.

Hunt paid him and Hal offered him a supply of provisions. Napo smiled his thanks but refused.

"Me eat," he said, tapping his bow. He could get what food he needed from river and forest.

After helping to push off the boat he lingered on the shore as if sorry to see his new friends go. As the canoe was swiftly borne downstream he called some sort of a goodbye in his own language and started to climb the steep, rocky slope beside the waterfall.

At the top of the fall he turned and waved, then was gone.

It seemed foolish for three men to feel lonely when one had gone. They still looked back at the edge of the waterfall. Napo was the only one of their party who had really known this jungle. Now they were starting into country from which no white man had ever come back.

Roger was the first one to snap out of it; he was not old enough to realize how much it meant. He had more confidence in his father and brother than they had in themselves.

"I think Nosey wants something to eat," he said. Because of its prominent proboscis and its way of poking its inquisitive trunk into everything and everybody, the little tapir had been nicknamed Nosey. "What does a tapir eat?"

"All sorts of leaves and shoots and juicy vegetable matter," Dad said. "But a baby tapir should have milk. Since there is no milk, you might try some very tender grass." They passed close enough to the bank for Roger to seize a handful of fresh young grass and he offered this dainty to Nosey.

Nosey turned up his nose at it, or would have, except that the nose was of the permanently turned-down variety.

"Now, you're not going to be a problem child," John Hunt said reprovingly. Nosey at once proceeded to be a problem child by attempting to jump overboard, but was drawn back by the harness that had been made for him out of lianas.

"Perhaps we'll just have to let him live on his own fat for a while until he decides to eat," said Dad, and he turned to something of more immediate importance. He took out pad, pencil and compass.

"Going to map the river?" Hal asked in some excitement.

"Yes. Would you like to help?"

"Let me do it and you help," Hal ventured. He could

think of nothing more thrilling than to chart the course of an unknown river.

John Hunt smiled indulgently. "Well, I'm sure you can do it," and he passed over the materials.

Hal's eyes sparkled. "Now, we begin with the fall – right? Has it a name?"

"Not that I know of."

"What shall we call it?" He thought of it as they had seen it, with Napo on its crest waving goodbye. "Napo Falls. How's that?"

"As good as anything."

Hal made a mark at the top of the pad and wrote "Napo Falls". Then he began to trace the river. The paper was blue lined in squares, each representing a square mile. Hal estimated the distance back to the waterfall and the distance forward to the next large bend. He consulted the compass to get the direction correct. He had often watched surveyors at work.

"I wish we had all the proper instruments," he said.

"They'd be too bulky to take on a trip like this. If we come out with a roughly accurate map, that will encourage surveying parties to come in and complete the job."

Every time a hill or mountain could be seen it went down on the map together with its estimated altitude.

Marginal notes recorded stands of trees, particularly those of commercial importance such as cinchona and rubber trees, or trees valuable because of their timber.

Dad continually contributed suggestions out of his former experience, but Hal made the map.

The changing width of the river was indicated, and the depth of it, and the character of the various rapids.

Hal realized what it felt like to be a real pioneer. All future travellers on this river would owe something to him for the work he was doing today. He felt his responsibility and did his job with all possible care.

So the day slid by without much thought of enemies who might be lurking behind this screen of jungle. Camp was made on a small island. It would be hard for any Indians to come to it without being detected.

Meat from the tapir shot the night before was the chief item on the dinner menu. It was very good, much like beef, but with just enough of a pork taste to give it a tang.

During the night they thought they heard drums, but were not sure, so great was the animal din of the forest.

Another day of canoeing and mapping followed and still there was no sign of Indians, and still Nosey refused to eat. Once in a while he whimpered like a baby or a pup. They began to worry about him. If he kept on this way he would never see a zoo.

The difficulty was solved, but in a way that nearly wrecked the expedition.

Rounding a bend, they saw two goats standing knee-deep in a natural meadow. One of them was a nanny and carried a full bag.

"Wild goats," cried Roger. "There's some milk for Nosey."

The goats stood quite still, eyeing the boat.

"They can't be wild," said Hal. "If they were they would run."

"But there's no village around."

"Perhaps it's farther back in the woods."

"Well, anyhow," suggested Roger, "on that beach would be a good place for lunch."

The suggestion seemed good and they ran the canoe ashore and took out a few provisions. From the beach they could not see the goats since a high bank came between.

After eating they lay half dozing on the beach. Hal and his father did not notice when Roger took a bottle from the kit and climbed the bank.

Some fifteen minutes later they were brought to their feet by a piercing yell and the whiz of an arrow. Roger came tumbling down the bank clutching a bottle of milk.

"Quick! They're shooting at me."

The three were in the canoe in a flash and paddling into midstream. The strong current came to their rescue. Another arrow whirred after them but fell short. In a moment they were around a bend and breathed more freely.

But their relief was short-lived. They saw a log canoe in a cove. They had not gone five hundred feet past it when three Indians ran to the boat, leaped in, and came in hot pursuit.

Mischievous Roger had some belated regrets. The three Hunts bent to their paddles as if their lives depended upon it — as they quite possibly did.

They were three against three. But the Indians were familiar with the river and knew the best channels. And they had had more experience in paddling a log canoe.

The Hunts held the lead for a mile, then were slowed up by a scraping over a hidden sand bar. The other canoe was fairly flying over the water. The Indians made a living thing out of it.

One of them laid down his paddle and took up a bow. It was seven feet long. He stood up in the boat to bend it and string the long, evil-looking arrow.

Twang — whiz. The arrow embedded itself in the

gunwale of the Hunt canoe and the feather on the end of it whirred like a rattlesnake's tail.

Dad was not one to forget his job as a collector, even at a bad moment like this. He pulled out the arrow and placed it safely inside the boat.

"Some museum will like that."

Dad tried a show of friendship. He lifted both hands and smiled. But Roger's theft had rather spoiled the friendship technique. The Indians responded with angry shouts and another arrow. This one caught John Hunt in his upraised right arm. A contortion of pain passed over his face.

That was enough for Hal. He lifted his Savage repeating rifle, loaded with high-power, flat-shooting .300 cartridges, famous for their "smashing power".

All right, now was the time for them to smash.

"Don't kill them," warned his father.

"I won't." He levelled his gun at the canoe to strike it just below the water line. The powerful rifle ripped the jungle silence with its roar. The canoe and its howling occupants were hidden by a shower of spray. When it cleared, the canoe was sinking and the Indians were splashing their way towards shore.

"Can I help you, Dad?"

"No. You and Roger keep paddling. But first pass the salt."

Hal gave his father a startled look. Had the old man gone crazy?

"Yes, I mean it, give me that can of salt."

Hunt had pulled out the arrow and laid it beside the other. He noticed that the tip was covered with a black gum. That was curare poison. He knew, because he carried some of it in his own kit – it was useful to the hunter.

He pulled up his sleeve. The arrow wound was slight. But the poison was enough to cause death in a few minutes. Animals and Indians who did not consume salt succumbed to it quickly. Salt-eating white men might succeed in throwing off its effect.

Hunt slashed the wound larger with the point of his hunting knife. Then he briskly rubbed salt into it. He filled his mouth with salt and washed it down with a little water.

"Sorry to leave all the work to you," he said as he stretched himself out in the bottom of the boat.

"Would you like to lie up on shore?"

"No, no. Keep going. I'll be all right."

Curare breaks the connection between the nerves and the muscles. It leaves the muscles limp. And that is why this deadly invention of the Amazon Indians is now being used to good purpose in European and American hospitals in cases where the tension of the muscles must be relaxed. But it is easy to go too far. Whether Hunt had taken in enough of the poison to relax him for ever, even he did not know.

The muscles in the head and neck were the first to be affected. He could not move his head. The numbness spread down over his chest to the between-rib muscles and the diaphragm, which take care of respiration. As they became faint, he had trouble in breathing. He would rather just stop. He kept manfully at it, knowing it was his only chance to hang onto life.

The boys did not realize the seriousness of the situation. It was just as well, since there was nothing they could do. Their best service was to put distance between them and an angry Indian village.

79

9
The Chase

Boom-boom-boom-boom, came an ominous sound through the forest.

"Drums!" Hal exclaimed. "Those Indians must really be annoyed."

He glanced back anxiously but there was no canoe in sight – as yet. He and Roger made the water churn with their paddles. The current helped, but unfortunately it would help their pursuers too.

Nosey made a whinnying sound like that of a pony.

"Just be patient, little river horse," Roger said. "No time for you now."

He pushed the bottle of fresh goat's milk into a shady spot, sopped his handkerchief in the river, and threw it over the bottle to keep it cool.

Hal did not forget his map, but no sketching and noting were ever done so swiftly. He begrudged every moment away from his paddle.

There was another sound now, the roar of a rapid. Ahead, green and white waves leaped in the sunlight. They were beautiful, but black rocks showed their sullen faces beneath them.

There was no time to get out and look the situation over. No time to pick and choose channels. The boat flew at the rapid as if it would conquer it by mere speed.

The current dipped and became a green toboggan. It hissed like a snake and there was something snakelike in the way it glided swiftly down and wound between the rocks.

There was a louder roar and Roger, in the bow froze as he saw what lay ahead. If Hal at stern paddle could manoeuvre the boat through this he was even better than Roger thought him.

The slope ended in a dive between two great boulders. If the flying arrow of a boat were steered just a trifle to the right or left there would be a resounding crash and nothing but splinters left on the Pastaza.

Roger poised his paddle to be ready to stave off if necessary. But would the paddle break if it struck the rock at this speed, or would it pull out of his hand or run into his chest and throw him out of the boat?

Luckily he did not have to find out. The canoe made a clean cut between the boulders and then smacked into the waves at the base of the incline. It was tossed up as lightly as if it had been a feather instead of a hollowed log, then came down to smash its way through the backlashers.

The noise of the torrent was like the thunder of a train going over a bridge and the spray was blinding. What looked like a white curtain blocked their path. They tore a hole in it and found themselves in small choppy waves like afterthoughts, and then in smooth, swift water fanning out into a quiet pool.

If ever there was a time when they would have liked to stop and rest and think, it was then. But they kept their paddles racing because, as the thunder of the rapids died away, they could once more hear the drums.

"Good work," said Dad weakly from the bottom of the boat.

Hal looked back. "I hope the Indians take time to carry around that." Then he made a sudden exclamation and dug in his paddle. "There they come."

A canoe was poised at the top of the slide. With a whoop that sounded painfully like a war whoop the Indians sent their craft down the chute, skilfully dodged the rocks, then disappeared in the churning foam.

The boys yelled with delight as they saw the boat come out of the lather upside down. Three dark bobbing objects marked the Indians. This was something to see, and Dad tried to raise his head, but it was no go.

Why had the Indians been capsized? Certainly they were skilful canoeists. Hal meditated that the cargo had helped to ballast his own boat through the rough water. And his father's weight low down along the bottom had contributed to success.

Another canoe now appeared at the top of the rapid. This one made the descent safely. Still another canoe followed. It rode on its beam for a tantalizing moment but righted itself in time.

It was some satisfaction that both canoes turned back to rescue the swimmers and their boat. Hal and Roger made full use of this intermission. The dugout slid around a curve into a long, straight stretch that seemed to end in a mountain. As they came closer a slit appeared. The river vanished between two vertical cliffs.

Here was a new problem. Hal was aware that a river usually narrows and speeds up in a gorge. There are not likely to be beaches or banks and the chances of making a landing in case of danger are very slim. Once in a gorge you can't get out of it except at the other end.

The right thing to do would be to stop and reconnoitre. He glanced back. The Indians had collected their forces and were charging down the river, three canoes abreast.

Hal steered for the mouth of the canyon. It was narrow and dark and the river slicked into it at high speed.

The Indians were only a hundred yards away now and coming full tilt. But there seemed to be confusion in their ranks. They were yelling in great excitement. They began to shoot but the arrows fell short. Just as the Hunts' boat entered the canyon's jaws, the pursuing canoes suddenly wheeled out of the current to the shelving shore.

Roger yelped with joy. "They're afraid to come on."

But an icy chill went down Hal's spine. It was not because of the cold shadow cast by the cliffs. If the Indians did not dare follow there must be something pretty bad ahead.

He strained his ears for the sounds of rapids. The stillness got on Hal's nerves. The river slid along rapidly without a ripple or a murmur. The cliffs were only thirty feet apart and rose sheer from the water. Their black forbidding faces were about two hundred feet high. Overhead was a narrow ribbon of blue sky that seemed very far away as if it belonged to another world.

"Ho-ho-ho!" yelled Roger, who wanted to hear the echoes. Hal jumped nervously. The sound was battered back and forth between the cliffs, rising and quickening

84

until it became a devilish rattle and then wailed away in a mournful whine down the canyon.

"Shut up!" said Hal irritably.

The canyon twisted and squirmed. At each turn Hal looked for trouble but there was none. The river was free of rocks, deep and oily smooth and in a tremendous hurry. Another turn. Now a breath of sound drifted up the canyon, but before he could decide whether it was made by water or wind it was gone. He looked up to see if the trees that lined the canyon's edge were blowing. They were stone still. Far above, several dozen scarlet ibis in a great crimson V flew across the blue ribbon. Perhaps they had made the sound.

Looking up to that sunlit blue was like looking out through the bars of a jail into a free world. This gorge was like a prison. Hal instinctively dug in his paddle and hurried the canoe along towards whatever danger there might be ahead. He was impatient to get it done with.

He shivered. The equator was nearby and yet it was cold between these black, sunless walls. He felt strangely alone and helpless. His father appeared to be asleep. Roger had no feeling of responsibility. He was trying to feed Nosey from the bottle of goat's milk. The little tapir slobbered noisily and each slobber came back from the walls like a handclap. The youngster's whimper was turned by the cliffs into a faint, cackling laugh.

Hal admitted to himself that he was having a bad case of the jitters. He wished that they had stayed out of this hellhole. It would have been better to fight the Indians.

But he knew this was not true. If they had killed some Indians the only result would have been to bring hundreds more upon their necks.

Again a sound drifted up the canyon, and as the canoe swept around a curve Hal hoped to see the gorge open out. Instead, it seemed to be closing in. The crests of the cliffs came closer together and large trees locked their branches across the chasm. Presently the rock ceiling was complete overhead. They were in a tunnel. Roger could not see to feed Nosey and looked up, bewildered.

The darkness deepened. Now Hal could not see the paddle in his hand. The black water and black walls were all one. It was useless to steer; the current must do the steering. If there happened to be a great rock in the middle of the current – well, it was just too bad.

No wonder the Indians had not followed. Hal had read of streams that disappear underground to become subterranean rivers. He remembered a story under the title, *The River of No Return*. It was not a comforting thought.

"Holy smokes! What's that?" cried Roger.

"What?"

"Something flying around us."

The air was pulsating with the beat of wings. "Must be bats," Hal said. They were on every side. There must be hundreds of them. Hal pulled his head lower to avoid them although he knew that the radar-like equipment of the bat enables it to fly in pitch darkness without striking anything – unless it wants to.

Unless it wants to. Suppose these were some of the vampire bats that were so common in the American tropics and that liked nothing better than to pierce the skin of a warm-blooded animal, such as man, and lap up blood. But he tried to tell himself that they would not attack anything in swift motion.

Now the cavern was filled with the fine squeaking of the bats. But under their high soprano there was developing a deep baritone.

That was the sound of water. It grew into a thunder, but it was still distant. Could there be an underground waterfall? Would they be carried blindly over it and dashed to pieces on unseen rocks?

Hal had been taught to believe that he was master of his fate. But now he and his companions were being whirled along to an unknown destiny and there was not one thing he could do about it.

The river seemed to make a sudden turn and the canoe scraped against a wall. Hal clutched at the wall and his hand ploughed through bats clinging to its surface. The current pulled the boat away and it hurried on.

But now there was a faint gleam of light, enough to make out the wheeling and swooping of the bats. With the growing light, there grew also the thunder of water ahead.

Hal's spirits leaped. "We're getting out of it!" He did not mind the increasing thunder. Anything was better than that black rat-trap.

There were some cracks in the ceiling now. It was good to get a glimpse of blue sky — it seemed an age since he had seen it last.

Another curve, and both boys whooped as the roof burst asunder and the cliffs fell away into rocky slopes. The light was blinding. The fresh air smacked them hard in the face and it was full of a powdery spray. The river was churning up into white waves.

Roger peered ahead. "Where does it go?" The river seemed to meet the sky and end right there. The boat was only a few dozen yards from this end and running like a racehorse. There was no chance of making the shore.

"Waterfall!" shouted Hal, but the din was so great that he could not be heard. Roger glanced back to see that his brother was paddling furiously, and he did the same. Their only chance was to shoot the canoe over the brink so fast that it would come down on its keel rather than on its nose. Even so, they were in for a smashed canoe if there happened to be rocks below.

Roger yelled like a demon. This was fun, as long as it lasted. Hal thought only of the sleeping or unconscious form in the bottom of the boat. This was a mean spot for a sick man.

The canoe shot out into space. Hal, at the last moment, reversed his stroke and backed water strongly to hold the bow up. Then came a falling sensation. They seemed to fall and fall, and could hardly believe it later when they saw that the drop was only about ten feet. But that much of a fall is plenty in a canoe!

The prayer that the canoe would not split on a rock was answered – it soused into deep water, still right side up. Hal relaxed, Roger relaxed. That was their mistake. A strong side eddy with choppy waves upset the boat in a twinkling.

Even as it went over Hal leaped to get hold of his father. Gripping him, he went down and then came up to battle with the current, which was making a determined effort to smash them on the rocks.

Roger, swimming like an eel, struggled to right the boat and bring it to shore. The white tops of waves tumbled down upon his head time and again but he always came up to give a yell of defiance and to yank the boat closer to shore.

When he reached it he found Hal and his father laid out on the bank like corpses awaiting burial. Hal was done in. The nervous reaction from the weird ride through the tunnel and the plunge over the fall had left him cold and shaking. The impact of the water had roused John Hunt and his eyes were open but he was too weak to move.

The kit, lashed into the canoe, had made the trip safely. Roger unlashed it and put it out on the rocks to dry.

Then he suddenly thought of Nosey. Where was the little tapir? The end of its leash was still tied to the thwart. Roger followed the leash down to the river's edge and into a pool behind a big rock.

There was Nosey, having the time of his life. He rolled and dived and snorted like a baby sea lion. Roger let him enjoy himself.

Among the rocks were the battered hulks of two dugout canoes. There was nothing to show whether the canoeists had been Indians, or other adventurers whose attempt to explore the Pastaza had ended at this point.

John Hunt also saw the wrecks.

"Hal," he said weakly, "you took that fall like a veteran. And incidentally, thanks for pulling me out."

But Hal, in the warm comfort of the sun, was fast asleep.

10
Mystery of the Vampire Bat

There was not much sleep that night.

The camp had visitors. Not Jivaro Indians – though they were half expected. The visitors were of a much more strange and horrifying sort.

Roger, already covered with mementoes of his bout with the army ants, again proved to be an appetizing morsel. Some people are possessed of a chemical composition that attracts hungry creatures. Roger unfortunately belonged in this group.

They had not been in their hammocks more than an

hour when Roger woke. He could not tell what had wakened him. There was a slight pain in the big toe of his right foot. He put his hand on it and felt something wet.

He turned on his flashlight. His hand was smeared with blood, and so was the toe. The blood continued to pour out of a hole about an eighth of an inch in diameter that was as neatly bored as if it had been made with a gimlet.

"Hey! I'm being eaten alive," he yelled.

Hal woke from a dream that cannibals were making a meal of his younger brother. He was a little disgusted when he saw the small hole.

"You probably got your foot against a thorn."

"Don't be a dope. There are no thorns here. Besides, why does it keep on bleeding?"

Dad spoke from his hammock. "Listen!"

Somewhere above was a canopy of beating wings, hundreds of them.

Suddenly Hal remembered the bats of the caverns.

"Oh, no!" he exclaimed. "This is too good to be true."

"What's good about it?" retorted Roger, sopping blood with his handkerchief.

"They must be vampire bats. The London Zoo will pay two thousand dollars for one."

"I must see that," said Dad, struggling to get out of his hammock.

"Stay where you are. I'll bring it to you." And Hal took hold of the pedal specimen and nearly dragged Roger out of his hammock in order to show Dad the punctured foot.

"What am I, a guinea pig?" wailed Roger, but no one was paying much attention to his complaints.

"Think of it, Dad," Hal cried. "If we could only get one! You remember what Dr Ditmars told us – the one he got was the first ever exhibited in the Bronx Zoo. And it died after only a few months. And the London Zoo has never had one."

"Bandage his toe until it stops bleeding," Dad said. "Then put on iodine. You'll live," he assured Roger.

"But how are we going to catch one?" wondered Hal. "Of course we could wait until one bites Roger again and then grab it."

Roger glared at his brother. "Be your own guinea pig," he snapped. And when his toe was bandaged he covered himself completely with his blanket, face and feet included. "Now let the ugly little beasts try to get at me."

If it was a dare, it was soon taken up. The camp was quiet only a few minutes before there was another yelp from Roger.

The boy had forgotten to put the blanket under him as well as over. An exploring bat had discovered a slight rip in the seat of his trousers and had bitten him through the meshes of the hammock. But, again, the visitor had escaped.

Despairing of making a meal on Roger, the greedy little monsters were turning their attention to Dad and Hal. Dad had already had a caller. Before it could make an incision he grabbed at it, but it was off and away before his fingers closed.

Hal got a small hand net from the kit.

"Now I'm going to set a trap for them."

"What will you use for bait?"

"Me," laughed Hal, a little uneasily. "If William Beebe could do it, I can."

Beebe, the well-known naturalist, had deliberately exposed his arm and waited for a vampire to bite him. The creature landed lightly and began to make an opening. Beebe's imagination played tricks with him and he thought he felt blood flowing. He tried to seize the bat but it eluded him. Examining the arm, he found that he had interrupted the bat too soon – only a slight scratch had been made and there was no blood.

Hal determined that he was going to stick it out, no matter how it felt. The methods of the vampire bat had always been a dark mystery that was only now beginning to be cleared up by such men as Ditmars and Beebe.

The vampire had always been call a "bloodsucking bat". Ditmars had proved that it does not suck blood, but laps it up as a cat laps milk. There had been legends that the bat fans its victims to sleep with its wings. Others had it that the bat hovers over the body instead of alighting when it bites.

Hal would find out whether these stories were true. He stretched out his bare arm and lay very still. For a long time nothing happened.

Then the beat of wings seemed to come closer. Finally he felt a very light pressure on his chest, as if a bat had landed there. It was as light as a breath and if he had been asleep he would have never noticed it.

There was no sensation for a while. He could hardly bear the suspense. He wanted to leap up and beat the air to drive away the loathsome creature that wheeled around him.

Then he was aware of a slight tickling on his wrist. That was the the only sign that a landing had been made there. He was not even sure that he felt it.

But the tickling now seemed to be going up his arm to the elbow. Or it might be just the night breeze blowing over his arm. He couldn't be sure.

For a while there was nothing. Then his arm, near the elbow, had a slight tingling sensation as if it were going to sleep. This discovery excited Hal greatly. Scientists had often speculated as to how a bat could cut a hole without the victim feeling it. It was believed possible that the bat's saliva contained a local anaesthetic which numbed the spot where the bite was to be made. What Hal felt seemed to bear out this idea.

Like Beebe, Hal imagined that the hole was cut and the blood was flowing. He resolutely lay still. There was one thing sure – the actual cutting of the hole could not be felt, nor the lapping up of the blood. Or else the bat had flown away. He couldn't tell.

Perhaps he was just fancying the whole thing. But no, now he could really feel something – the very faint sensation of warm blood flowing down over the part of the arm that had not been drugged.

He felt he had learned enough for one lesson. He must capture the little blood drinker before it satisfied itself and flew away.

With all the force at his command he swung the net across his body and down upon his elbow, then twisted the handle smartly so that anything caught in the net could not escape.

He reached for his flashlight. Yes, he had not been just imagining things. His arm was a gory sight. He did not bother with it but looked at the net. A devilish-looking creature struggled in its meshes.

"I've got it!" he yelled. "I've got! Dad, look!"

An extraordinary face leered out of the net. Hal thought he had never seen a face more evil – except one, and his memory went back for an instant to the face of the man who had followed him that night in Quito.

The old legend that had given birth to the name of this creature came back to his mind. "Vampires" were supposed to be ghosts that came out of their graves at night to suck the blood of human beings. This superstition had been the basis of that terrible play, *Dracula*.

Certainly this bat embodied all the horror of the old legend. It was a thing of the night, dark, sinister, with beady eyes full of hate peering out through overhanging fur. The ears were pointed like those generally pictured on Satan himself. The nose was flat and the underjaw projected like a prize fighter's.

"Looks like a cross between the devil and a bulldog," John Hunt whispered, for the face seemed too dreadful to be spoken of aloud.

But they were yet to see the worst. The bat opened its

mouth in a vicious snarl. The long nimble tongue with which it had been lapping up its dinner was covered with blood. The beast seemed very short on teeth, but those it had were terribly efficient. There were two long canines, one on each side.

But the really amazing teeth, the ones that had given the vampire its fabulous reputation, were in the front of the upper jaw. They were twin incisors, slightly curved and as sharp as needles. It was with these lances that the bat made its deep but painless incisions.

Besides blood, there was a sort of watery mucus in the mouth. If he ever got this bat to a laboratory he would have that secretion analysed to see if it contained any narcotic agent that puts the flesh to sleep, or anything that prevents blood from clotting.

He looked at his arm. The blood was still running from the hole. His father staunched it by tying a handkerchief tightly around it.

That was what often caused death, especially to small animals – not the bite of the vampire, but the continued flow of blood after the bat had finished feeding. Blood ordinarily clots in a short time. Did the saliva of the bat contain a chemical that prevent clotting?

That was something to find out.

The bat beat its wings, but the net was strong. While no stories could have overstated the ugliness of this creature, its size had been exaggerated. It had been confused with the great fruit bat which may measure two or three feet between wing tips. The span of this bat was only twelve inches and its body was about four inches long.

"Little, but oh my!" came from Roger.

If they could ever get this thing home, how many thousands of people would look at it with the same wonder and awe with which they were gazing at it now! Here was a creature barely known to science – at least the Hunts did not know of a zoo or animal collection in the world that now possessed a specimen. But could they get it back alive?

Hal had a distressing thought.

"How are we going to feed it?"

"I was wondering about that myself," his father admitted. "It has to have about half a cup of fresh blood every day."

They looked at each other, puzzled. Then Hal turned his gaze upon Roger.

"Not me!" cried Roger. He was really ready to believe that he was about to be offered up, a living sacrifice, to science. With an iodined hole in his toe and another in his rear, he felt that he had done enough for the advancement of knowledge.

"We won't call upon you," his father assured him.

"Except in case of emergency," Hal qualified. "And if you don't want that to happen you'd better unlimber your .22 and get at least one warm-blooded animal per day for Vamp."

The idea cheered Roger considerably. He loved to use his gun and only wanted a good excuse. This was it. He could hardly wait until morning.

Vamp spent the rest of the night in the net. In the morning, she – for in spite of her lack of feminine beauty she was identified as a member of the fair sex – was transferred to a cage that Hal had made from strips of bamboo.

Roger, who usually could think of nothing in the morning except eating, was off before breakfast into the woods with his Mossberg. It was a 15-shot automatic equipped with a scope. It was loaded with high-speed Long Rifle cartridges. Although the gun was light and its calibre was only .22, he had killed a big puma with it in Colorado.

Now he secretly hoped to get a shot at a *tigre*. But after a half hour of stalking, all he came upon was a ratlike capybara, and a little one at that. The capybara, when full grown, is three feet long and the world's largest rodent.

This one was no bigger than a wharf rat. He almost scorned to bother with it. But, thinking of Vamp, and his own breakfast, he let fly.

The result was rather astonishing. The little capybara seemed to emit a roar that shook the forest as it fell over dead. Roger was paralysed with surprise. Then there was a flash of black and yellow in the bushes behind the capybara and the disappointed *tigre* that had been stalking it bounded away through the brush.

When Roger saw the size, power and grace of the big animal he changed his mind about wanting to meet it with a .22.

Thankful that he had not wounded it and brought it tumbling out upon him, he took up the little rodent and walked back to camp, with frequent glances behind him.

Breakfast was served to Vamp inside her cage, which was shrouded in cloth in order to make it as dark as the caverns that had been her home during daylight hours.

After a time Hal peeked in but the cautious Vamp was still hanging upside down to the top of her cage.

The three explorers had their own breakfast. Then Hal took another look. The bat was poised like a great spider over the rodent and was feeding greedily but, disturbed by the light, immediately retreated again to the top of the cage.

In that flash, Hal had seen enough. It was true. The vampire was not a bloodsucker as most scientists supposed it to be. Its mouth had not touched the wound. He had seen its long, bluish-pink tongue darting out and in at the rate of about four times a second. The movement was so rapid that a continuous column of fluid spanned the gap from wound to mouth. It was the technique of a cat or dog, but at high speed.

And to think that this operation could be carried on so gently that a sleeping victim was not wakened, and one wide awake scarcely knew what was going on!

Late in that day's journey another prize was added to the animal-collectors' bag. Like the vampire, it was small in size but large in value. But it was quite unlike the bat in appearance. It was as lovely as the other creature was ugly.

Camp was being made for the night when Hal spied the little creature in a branch of a tree. It was only two or three inches long, except for the tail, and could not weigh more than four ounces. It was covered with soft, golden hair except around the eyes and mouth. There the skin was white and the little fellow looked as if he had kissed a flour barrel and were wearing a large pair of white spectacles.

"It's a pigmy marmoset," Hal called to his father. John Hunt had already been made comfortable in his hammock. He was gradually recovering from the effect of the curare.

"Get it with the blowpipe," he advised Hal.

Roger ran to the boat and got a blowgun that had been presented to them by the Jivaro chief. He brought also a quiver full of darts and a small bottle of curare.

Hal dipped the point of a dart into the curare so that it picked up only the slightest touch of the poison. Then he fitted the dart in the near end of the seven-foot-long bamboo tube. The butt end of the dart was wrapped in the cotton from the kapok tree, making a ball just the right size to fit snugly in the bore of the gun.

Hal raised the blowpipe, put his lips to the mouthpiece, and blew hard.

Fortunately the pigmy, as curious as most monkeys, was sitting very still, taking a keen interest in the proceedings. It made a perfect target. Even so, Hal expected to miss, for he was not adept with the blowpipe – but the dart struck the little fellow in the side.

He chattered excitedly, pulled it out, and threw it away. He started to climb through the tree. But the poison acted fast. He paused, tottered a little, and then fell. He did not check himself with his tail, for the marmoset is not prehensile.

Hal picked him out of the grass. Roger knew his role in this little drama and had the salt ready. Some of it was rubbed into the wound.

"He's just numbed a little," Hal said.

The marmoset began to stir in Hal's hands. Its eyes opened. At first dull, they gradually brightened. The golden plume of a tail began to switch about and some tentative remarks came from the funny white lips under the white-ringed eyes.

Roger was delighted. "Feeling better, Specs?" And it was so that the little fellow got his name.

"I think we'll find Specs a very interesting companion," John Hunt said. "Perhaps sometimes a little too interesting. The marmoset is one of the liveliest, most alert, and most curious of all the monkeys. Of course most of the varieties are larger than this one. The pigmy marmoset is the smallest monkey in the world. That's a point of distinction that should make it interesting to any collector. Do you know, Hal, I wouldn't be surprised if this is a new variety of the pigmy. If he is, they may give him your name, added to his own. Then he'll be *Hapale pygmaeus hunti*."

"Well, to us," said Hal, "he'll just be Specs Hunt."

Specs Hunt came to realize very quickly that he was a member of the Hunt family, and demanded all the privileges pertaining thereto. He was a gentle little fellow, made chirps like a bird, but leaps like an acrobat, and was all over everything all the time. He did not seem to have a streak of the meanness that sometimes characterizes a monkey. He was mischievous in a merry way, but handled himself with such squirrel-like lightness that he rarely upset or broke anything.

His greatest delight was to play with Charlie's long black hair. He would leap out of it at Nosey, the tapir, and land upon his back. But when Nosey tumbled overboard for a bath, taking Specs with him, Specs was loud in disapproval and would clamber back into the boat and make straight for Roger, whom he had adopted as his special guardian.

He would climb inside Roger's shirt and lie there wet and cool against his skin until he dried.

It was going to be hard to part with Specs.

11
Noah's Ark on the Amazon

"The Amazon!" cried Hal, as the canoe swept around a curve and pointed its nose out into a far greater river, broad, swirling, and full of brown humps like lions' heads with manes flowing – mounds of water that hinted the power and speed of the current.

For five days they had followed the mysterious dotted line. When a new map was made that line would be solid. Hal completed his pencilled map by marking the juncture with the Amazon. Then he put the map carefully away in a waterproof bottle and placed the bottle in the waterproof medicine box. That map was one of the expedition's most cherished possessions.

The Amazon, greatest river on earth! Roger and his father were as excited as Hal. The other passengers seemed to share the excitement, or it may have been that they were only disturbed by the rolling and pitching of the little canoe.

The tapir whinnied, the marmoset chirped, and even the sleepy vampire in her dark cage squeaked in alarm. Only Charlie took the whole thing calmly. Hanging from his thwart, the mummified hero did not even deign to open his eyes. He merely nodded gravely.

"Is this really the Amazon?" Roger wanted to know.

"Yes and no," said his father. "But mostly yes. Look on your American Geographical map. You'll notice that the entire river from here to the Atlantic is called the Amazon. But in addition to that, each part of the river has a special name. Some people call this section the Marañon, and the next section the Solimoes. But it's all the Amazon."

"How soon do we build the raft?" enquired Roger eagerly.

The canoe had been the best vessel for shooting the rapids of the Pastaza, but no animals of any size could be collected and carried in a canoe. Besides, on these great waters, a canoe was none too safe. It had been decided that upon reaching the Amazon they would build a raft to transport their animals and themselves downstream.

Roger had even suggested the name for it. *Noah's Ark*.

"The sooner the better," Hunt said. "But we can't land here – the current is too strong. Let's watch for a cove."

The wind blew fresh from the far shore, a mile away. If it had not been for the current, they might have imagined themselves on a lake instead of a river. On the port side the near shore was a riot of flowering trees. Near the bank, waterfowl bobbed up and down in the ripples and went up in a cloud as the boat approached.

Roger reached for the shotgun. But the careening of the boat reminded him to be prudent.

Birds of all kinds, colours and calls adorned the forest. This was evidently a bird paradise. But the most astonishing bird was the jabiru stork, as tall as a man, which walked along the shore with the stately step of a king.

They rounded a point where the wild lashing of water sent the marmoset scurrying into Roger's shirt; then they slid into a calm bay. There was no current here except a lazy eddy that circled backwards around the curved shore. There was a gentle beach of pure sand, again reminding them of a lake shore. Behind this a gigantic ceiba tree threw its branches out to cover almost an acre of ground and beneath its shade nothing else dared to grow except light grass, forming a broad level park.

It was an ideal camping place for raft building. Nothing could be better for building purposes than the trunks of giant bamboo that grew in clumps near the shore, and lianas that would serve as cables to bind the craft together. It took them two days to build the raft. On both days they saw other rafts pass far out in the river and felt assured that they were on the right track. The Indians had found the raft to be the most practicable vessel for this particular stretch of the Amazon.

"But every raft has a house on it," exclaimed Roger. "Let's put a house on ours."

Accordingly a thatch hut with bamboo frame, reed walls and roof of palm leaves was constructed on the raft. Home sweet home afloat!

Now that there was a vessel large enough to accommodate them, two big animals joined the floating menagerie. One was a giant iguana, six feet long.

The huge tropical lizard was lying on a low branch when Roger discovered it. For once, Roger had been walking quietly, because he had been stalking a bird. Therefore, although he was only a dozen feet from the iguana, it was not disturbed.

In fact Roger was the more amazed of the two. He was used to seeing lizards a few inches or even a foot long, but this was unbelievable. It looked exactly like some pictures he had seen of prehistoric monsters.

It was green with brown stripes around its tail. It had a row of spikes down its back and another row of spikes under its chin. Its feet were like hands with long, thin, clawing fingers.

Roger slipped back to camp. "I think I saw something," he whispered.

"You *think* you saw it?"

"Well, I may be crazy," admitted Roger, "but it looked like an alligator up a tree."

"Alligators don't climb trees," his brother said scornfully.

"All right, come and see for yourself."

The three Hunts crept cautiously through the brush. The creature was still there, apparently half asleep.

"An iguana!" exclaimed Hunt. "Remember, you had an iguana steak at the Jivaro village. It's much prized by the Indians as food. They have an odd way of catching it. Let's try it. Get some noosing cord."

"I have some in my pocket," said Hal.

"Good. Make a noose and have it ready to slip over his head."

"But we can't just walk up to him and noose him, can we?"

"No. We have to sing to him first. And pet him."

The boys looked at their father suspiciously. He must be joking.

"That's the way the Indians do it," insisted Hunt. "The iguana is very susceptible to music, and likes to be stroked."

He picked up a stick. "Here, Hal, stroke him with the end of this. And you sing, Roger."

Roger was no singer and he began to make a sound that it was hard to believe would charm either man or beast. Hal stroked the rough skin, standing as far away as possible.

The iguana moved slightly, opened its eyes wider, and turned its head to examine the visitors. Its jaws opened in what was perhaps just a lazy yawn but Roger was so startled by the array of sharp teeth that he stopped singing.

"They can give you a mean bite," Hunt said. "But he won't bite if we handle him gently. Sing, Roger, sing." So Roger sang and Hal stroked.

"Gently, gently," warned their father. "No zoo will take him without a tail. If you startle him, he'll lose it."

Roger stared. "Lose his tail? Just the way those little lizards do up home?"

"Just the same. All right, Hal, I think he's ready for the noose. Let me tie it to the end of your stick."

Hunt fastened the noose to the stick, then very warily lowered it before the iguana's nose. Every time there was the slightest movement he stopped and waited. Then, as softly as a caress, the noose was passed over the animal's head and slowly drawn tight.

"Got him!" yelled Roger.

"Quiet. Remember the tail."

Very gently Hunt began to pull. At first there was no response. Then the iguana slowly got under way, let itself sluggishly down to the ground, and allowed its captor to lead it into camp. Once it made a rush at Hal's heels, champing its jaws in terrifying fashion. It was half led, half lifted onto the raft.

"Now I suppose I have to get food for it," guessed Roger. "What does it eat?"

"Almost anything. Tender leaves and fruits, small birds, little animals."

And Roger went foraging.

The other new passenger was no less unique. It also was six feet long – but up and down rather than horizontally. A jabiru stork like the one they had seen upon approaching the camp site was attracted by some freshly caught fish that Hal had left in a pail on the beach. From the shadow of the big tree Hal watched quietly.

The great bird, high up on its thin legs like tall stilts, looked down gravely into the pail. Jabirus always look as if they are meditating deeply in spite of the fact that they have nothing on their minds but fish. Their shoulders are hunched and their heads bowed.

This solemn visitor seemed to think it all over and to decide that scooping up fish out of a pail was easier than hunting them in the river.

He was truly a majestic bird. His great body was covered with pure white feathers. His head was a glossy black, and there was a handsome red ring around his throat. He raised his wings slightly and Hal estimated that when they were fully spread they would measure seven feet from tip to tip. He could already see this greatest of all the world's storks walking through some zoological garden to the wonder and admiration of thousands of visitors.

Solemnly the great body teetered on its two slender supports and the foot-long bill darted into the pail. It was odd to see a bird that looked so wise and old make such a sudden movement. The fish disposed of, the stork resumed its air of great wisdom and stalked slowly down the beach.

Hal was helpless. He thought of lassoing the bird but despaired of getting close enough before the great feathered aeroplane would take to flight. He would have to let it go.

But he believed the tall visitor would come back, having learned how easy it is to get dinner out of a pail.

He replenished the pail with more live fish and left it exactly where it had been. He drove in four stakes and to the tops of them fastened the four corners of a net so that it spread like a roof about eight feet above the pail. He triggered the net with a slip cord that ran along the ground back to his retreat under the tree.

He had almost given up hope that day when, in the long light of the setting sun, the not-so-wise old stork came slowly stalking along the beach. He stopped twenty feet away to examine the pail and the net above it. This required thought. He stood on one leg – miraculously keeping his balance – tucked the end of the beak into the feathers on his breast, and meditated.

Finally reassured by the fact that neither the pail nor the net moved, he walked slowly under the canopy, eyed the contents of the pail for a moment, and then plunged.

At the same instant Hal jerked the slip cord and the net fell. Alarmed, the bird flew up. This action was not a bit wise for it only served to entangle him more securely in the net. In its meshes his toes, wing tips, and beak were all caught. He continued to thrash about. White feathers flew like snowflakes.

Before long those powerful wings would break the net. Roger and Dad were also witnesses to this experiment, and John Hunt now suggested, "Better get in there fast with the foot rope."

Hal ran up with the rope. Roger was not one to be left out of a game like this and he succeeded in getting in a spot where he was given a hard clout in the stomach by one of the bird's feet.

But during the instant while the foot was extended, Hal succeeded in getting a noose over it.

"The net is tearing! Hang on!" he yelled, as the stork burst through the net and soared up into the air. For a moment it looked as if both Hal and Roger would be carried away in the fashion of Sinbad the Sailor borne aloft by the roc. But their combined weight was too much even for the great aviator. They managed to get their end of the rope to the raft and tie it to a log.

The bird rose fifty feet until it was checked by the taut rope. Then it flew round and round in tight circles. The boys retreated from sight in order to give their captive a chance to recover from his surprise and fright.

But a jabiru stork has too much dignity to remain frightened long. Gradually the bird circled lower and finally lit on the raft. After wagging his great bill from side to side as if to say, "Well, I never!" he seemed to reflect, "I must remember that I am a philosopher and little things like this can't disturb me."

He collected himself, preened his ruffled feathers, shifted

his weight to one foot and tucked the other away, hunched his shoulders, poked his beak into his beard, and mused on the silly ways of men.

The banks of the Amazon would have been lined with astonished people if there had been any people to line them, as *Noah's Ark* sailed seawards with its extraordinary passenger list: tapir, vampire, marmoset, iguana, jabiru, three specimens of homo sapiens and a mummy. But this was only a beginning.

John Hunt was captain, Hal was first mate, and Roger was steward. It was Roger's business to feed the menagerie. That would have been simpler if they had all been willing to eat the same things. But he had a lot of fussy diners. Nosey preferred milk, but was beginning to accept leaves and shoots, Vamp wanted fresh blood, Specs was not content to eat vegetable matter like other monkeys but demanded insects, the giant iguana loved bulbs and blossoms, and for fish-eating Stilts every day was Friday.

The crew usually spent the night on board, moored to some island. The hut made a good bedroom. The hammocks were strung diagonally from corner to corner. They criss-crossed. Roger's was nearest to the roof, Hal's just below it, and their father's near the floor.

119

When Roger wished to descend, he stepped upon his brother and then his father. This amused him and he found reason for coming down frequently during the night with the excuse that he heard something strange and wanted to investigate.

Hal grew weary of being a stepping-stone, and plotted revenge. One night when his brother was sound asleep Hal unhooked one end of the boy's hammock, carried it out the side of the hut which had been left open, and lashed it to a tree on the bank. Roger was suspended over the water. In due time Roger awoke and prepared to torment his companions as usual. But this time he thought he would pretend to fall out of his hammock. He would come down on Hal with a terrific plop and scare the wits out of him. Hal would think that a jaguar had landed on him.

He eased himself to the edge of his hammock, balanced a moment, then let himself go.

There was a terrific plop, but not on Hal's chest. And the yell that rent the night was not Hal's but Roger's. It was muffled by a bubbling sound as he went below the surface of the Amazon.

Hal lay chuckling. Dad, awakened by the yell, leaped out of his hammock.

120

"Roger, is that you? Hal, I thought I heard Roger."

"Yes, I heard him too," said Hal, choking. "I think he went out."

Another burbling yell informed them of Roger's position and Dad was out in a flash to help him.

"A crocodile's got me," wailed Roger.

Hal stopped chuckling and tumbled out in a hurry. It was his turn to be scared. What fool thing had he done? This river was full of crocodiles as well as razor-toothed cannibal fish which could strip off all the flesh from a bather in a few moments. You might go in fifty times and not be attacked – but there was always the chance.

He pulled his hunting knife from its sheath as he ran outside. "I'll show that croc what's what!" He remembered what he had been told to do in case of a hand-to-hand encounter with a crocodile – gouge out its eyes.

He could dimly make out Roger in the water. He dived in and clutched Roger's legs, expecting to find them in the jaws of the crocodile. He found no monster but only a half-submerged log.

Roger had never really thought it was a crocodile. But now that he felt his legs gripped he was sure that a crocodile or perhaps even an anaconda had him in its toils. His terrified yells brought his father diving to the rescue and the three Hunts grappled madly with each other while the marmoset chirped, the bat squeaked, but the great stork was too far gone in wisdom and slumber even to open one eye or to put down his tucked-up foot.

To warm chilled bodies, a fire had to be built on the six-inch-deep bed of dirt that served as a fireplace in one corner of the hut. Then the crew retired once more, each grumbling that the whole business was the fault of the others.

Even solemn Stilts was disturbed the next day as the raft went in wild career down a series of rapids. Probably if a prize were given to the worst vessel in which to shoot rapids it would be awarded to the raft.

Noah's Ark was a bedlam of animal and human noises as it plunged into terrifying white waves among black rocks. It was impossible for three men to watch all four corners and every few seconds one corner or another was stuck on a boulder. Then the raft spun around as if a giant hand were twirling it. Somebody had to jump overboard to lift the logs free.

"Rock dead ahead!" cried Roger. There was no chance of avoiding it since there was another rock to the left and one to the right. The Hunts tried to delay their rush with poles and paddles, but it was no use. Hal's pole snapped in two.

The raft seemed doomed. It would surely be broken to pieces. The animals would be scattered and lost.

The rock struck the raft square in the middle of the forward deck. It was fortunate that the raft builders had not had nails or bolts with which to make a rigid vessel. The bamboo logs were only lashed together with lianas. The centre logs yielded, slid up over the rock, and something like a camel's hump passed along the raft and came out at the stern end.

For once, the stork had to put both feet down to keep his balance. The raft hung together but the strain on the hut was too much, and the thatch roof parted. No one minded that. None of the valuable animals had been lost.

Then the raft was teetered wildly this way and that until the disgusted stork took to flight. Forward he flew to the full length of his fifty-foot line and it looked exactly as if the great bird that is supposed to bring babies had decided that all the other passengers on the raft were innocents whom he must guide to safety.

When still water was reached he returned to the raft, looked from one to another of his companions, and made sarcastic little remarks deep in his throat.

Only one or two rafts were seen each day and there were rarely any Indian villages along the banks.

And then, one morning, a city!

After they had been seeing nothing but jungle for days, it seemed as big and as lively as New York. It was Iquitos (pronounced ee-kee-tose).

It was their last outpost before plunging into the deeper jungle of the Amazon. They tied the raft up to a pier. Hundreds of river boats were loading or unloading rubber, tobacco, cotton, timber, ivory nuts and Brazil nuts.

John Hunt stayed on board to guard their property while Hal and Roger eagerly set out to explore the streets. It was a frontier town with sawmills, shipyards, cotton gins, machine shops, and distilleries that produced rum from sugar cane juice. They passed a custom house, municipal palace, and a motion picture theatre showing pictures that they had seen years before on Long Island.

Following their father's instructions, they went in to call on the United States Consul. He had a cablegram for John Hunt.

Hal took it with a sense of foreboding. They almost ran back to the raft.

Dad opened the envelope and unfolded the message.

Hal thought of the cablegram received in Quito – would this also be a threat from some mysterious enemy?

When Dad looked up, Hal knew that something was seriously wrong.

"Boys," Dad said, "we've got to go home!"

12

Disaster

Hal took the radiogram. He saw that it was from his mother.

ALL BUILDINGS EXCEPT HOUSE DESTROYED BY FIRE ANIMALS BURNED TO DEATH ENTIRE COLLECTION LOST MUST BE WORK OF INCENDIARIES POLICE BAFFLED ANONYMOUS THREAT TO BURN HOUSE ALSO WHAT SHALL I DO

So this was the sequel to the warning in the first message:

AFFAIRS AT HOME WILL REQUIRE YOUR ATTENTION

"There's nothing we can do but get back there as fast as we can," said Dad.

He looked beaten. Nearly everything he owned had been wiped out. His animal collection was his livelihood. And to a man who loved animals, it was painful to think of them trapped in flaming buildings and burned to death. And now, this menace to their own home — perhaps to his wife as well.

Hal's thoughts were following a slightly different line.

"Who could have done it?" he wondered, and his thoughts went back to a face illuminated by a flashlight. "Dad, I told you about the man who followed me in Quito. You didn't take it very seriously — neither did I, then. But . . . do you think . . . ?"

"It's hard to see any connection between a tourist in Quito and a fire in Long Island."

"Yes, I guess you're right. But who could have it in for us?" Hal's analytical brain was working hard. "It can't be a personal grudge. You get along with everybody. You haven't any personal enemies. It can't be political — you don't mix in politics. There are lots of revolutionaries in these Latin American countries with axes to grind, but you've never had anything to do with that sort of thing. So it must be economic."

"What do you mean, economic?" Roger wanted to know.

"Someone stood to gain if Dad lost. Now, the only ones who could possibly gain if our business suffered would be our competitors – the other animal collectors. Most of the zoos and circuses and museums turn to us first. With us out of the market they will have to turn to somebody else."

"You're talking nonsense, Hal. None of the collectors would do this to me. I'm on the best terms with them."

"How about the biggest collector of all, except you?"

"You mean Griffis? Why, Griffis is an old friend. Besides, he sold out his business."

"Exactly," said Hal tensely.

"What are you driving at?"

"He sold it to a man named Sands. Do you know him?"

"Only by reputation," admitted John Hunt. "I think they call him Shark Sands – because he used to do some sharking in the South Seas. He seems to be a general roustabout. They say he ran a pearl-diving business and then got into gold mining in Australia. There was something about his working a mine that didn't belong to him and he got out just ahead of the law. He got into more trouble in the Philippines and skipped just in time to escape a murder charge. Oh, there are plenty of stories about Shark Sands. But he's no animal man. He wouldn't know a kangaroo from an elephant. He hasn't either the knowledge or the honesty to make a success of this business."

"Right," said Hal. "And that's exactly why he has to win by foul means."

John Hunt brushed away the suggestion impatiently. "You have a healthy imagination, Hal. But the important thing right now is to get home. A plane leaves here Tuesday, Thursday and Saturday. That means there's one tomorrow morning. We'll be on it."

And he strode uptown to make reservations.

Hal lay awake most of the night, thinking. In the morning over coffee he said, "Dad, you can cancel one of those reservations."

"What do you mean?"

"I mean I'm going to stay on the job here. Don't you see that what this – whoever it is – wants most is to make us call off this expedition? There's nothing he'd like better than to see us all come trotting home. He destroyed our animals – the last thing he'd like to see would be a new Amazon collection in the market. We can't let him beat us. Of course you have to go. I can handle this thing alone. I'll hire some men to help me."

"I wouldn't think of it," said John Hunt. "You're only a boy."

"But I'll stay with him. And I'll help him," said Roger.

John Hunt smiled at Roger's notion that his services would be valuable. "No, you are both too young to wrestle with this jungle."

"Listen, Dad," said Hal earnestly. "Your collection is gone. What are you going to do for money? The only way you can get back into business is to get a new collection. You've already invested a lot in this trip. If that fails, you are broke. Am I right?"

John Hunt reflected moodily. "I'm afraid you are."

"Think of Mom, think of all of us. The best thing you can do for us is to let Roger and me go through with this job."

"You don't seem to realize, Hal, that this is dangerous country. It's not Colorado."

Hal resorted to sarcasm. "So you think you have to take care of your little boys, don't you? I hate to rub it in, Dad, but I've got to remind you that you've been on the sick list half the time so far. Roger and I have done the work. If we could do it then we could keep on doing it."

"I couldn't let Roger. He's too scatterbrained."

Roger looked crestfallen. "I won't be scatterbrained. I'll promise to be as sensible as a judge."

"He'll mind what I say," said Hal, "won't you, Roger?"

Roger shot his brother a venomous look. But he swallowed the bitter pill. "Yes, I'll even take orders from Hal if you'll let me stay."

"All right," said John Hunt reluctantly. "But remember . . ." And he launched into detailed instructions to Hal. "And you," he said to Roger sternly, "no mischief!"

"Cross my heart!"

Dad flew on the morning plane.

13
Escape

The boys watched the plane until it was a mere speck in the sky.

Then they turned to each other with a solemn look. Suddenly they felt very much alone. They were two boys against the jungle. Hal's brave words of a little while ago seemed rather silly.

"We've got the easy end of it," Hal said, trying to reassure both himself and Roger. "We're only up against animals. He's up against an enemy who will stop at nothing."

"Well, if he'll stop at nothing," said Roger uneasily, "perhaps he'll even get at us down here."

"How could he?" scoffed Hal. "If Dad had thought that, he wouldn't have left us here. No, the danger spot right now is Long Island. Well, come on, we have a job to do." And they struck off towards the piers.

Hal was relieved to see that the raft was still there. He had somehow had a crazy notion that it would be stolen.

As they approached the raft the native policeman who had been asked to keep an eye on it came running up waving his arms and talking excitedly. Hal had studied

Spanish for two years and Portuguese for one in preparation for this trip. But he was not prepared for the weird hodge-podge of the two languages hurled at him by the policeman. He made out that during their absence a boat had arrived and the crew had set about untying the raft's cable from the pier and making it fast to the stern of the boat as if to take the raft in tow.

When the policeman objected, a man came out of the boat onto the pier and claimed that he was one of the owners of the raft. He just wanted to move it to a safer position. The policeman was polite, but suspicious and asked the stranger to wait until the others returned. There was quite an argument. Finally the stranger said he wouldn't wait, but would come back later, and off he went in his boat.

Hal tried to get a description of the stranger, but all that he could make out was that he was big, bad looking, and "no gentleman". And he spoke Spanish with an English accent.

Hal rewarded the faithful policeman with an extra coin and then went with him to the police station to lodge a complaint. Roger, armed to the teeth, and feeling very important, stayed to guard the raft.

The police were inclined to dismiss the matter as of no significance.

"Just somebody who made a mistake," said the chief, and added languidly, "However, we'll keep on the look-out for him."

It was quite evident that if anything was to be learned about the mysterious stranger, Hal would have to find it out for himself.

He went to the consul and told him the whole story.

"No one answering to that description has been here," the consul said. "Of course he might make a point of staying away. I don't know how you could find him or what good it would do you if you did. After all, you have nothing against him. He has done nothing actionable, nothing that could put him in jail. If the police arrested him they would have to free him and then he would be more determined than ever to do you down."

"What do you advise me to do?"

"Frankly, I'd advise you to follow your father's example. Hop on a plane and go home. Evidently there's a pretty sinister plot hatched up against you. We might protect you while you are in Iquitos, but as soon as you start down river there's nothing but jungle law. It's every man for himself – and you're only a boy."

The last words stung Hal. He was taller than the consul,

and stronger. Perhaps he didn't know as much but he would learn, and he would learn by taking any hard knocks the jungle had to give him.

"Thanks a lot," he said, "but we have a job to do and we're not going to let Shark Sands or any gunman of his stop us."

The consul looked up at him with a smile and put out his hand. "Well, you have plenty of spirit. Good luck!"

Hal returned to the pier to find Roger with his .22 in one hand, their father's Colt .45 in the other, and a bare hunting knife thrust through his belt. He stood on the pier with his feet braced apart and his lower jaw protruding, and he looked for all the world like Horatio defending the bridge.

The truth was the kid was scared to death. He was mightily relieved to see Hal.

"Did you find him?" he asked.

"No. But leave him alone long enough and I think he will find us."

"That's what I'm afraid of!"

They proceeded to carry out their father's instructions. The homemade raft had served well on the upper river, but for the wide and often stormy waters that they were about to enter, well-constructed boats were necessary.

More room would be needed if they were to take on more animals, especially if they happened to be large ones such as the jaguar and the anaconda. And to propel such boats, they would have to have a crew.

Leaving the friendly policeman on guard over the already valuable animal cargo, they explored the shipyards.

"Here it is," cried Hal at last. "Just what we're looking for."

"This really *does* look like Noah's Ark," laughed Roger.

It was the sort of craft that the Amazon people call a batalao. Fifty feet long, it had a deep cockpit, and was clinker-built – that is, the planks along its sides overlapped like the clapboards of a house. The whole afterpart of the vessel was covered with a roof that certainly looked as if Noah or some other early man had made it. The barrel-shaped thatch house called a toldo gave the whole thing the appearance of a gipsy van or a covered wagon. The vessel had a generously wide beam of about ten feet.

For the pilot who must manipulate the rudder there was at the stern a little platform perched so high that by standing on it he could look over the top of the house and see what was ahead. On the gunwales near the bow were oarlocks where four men might stand to the oars.

There was a sort of sidewalk the full length of each gunwale so that in shallow water the men might pole the boat by starting at the bow, digging their poles into the sand, and pushing while walking down the boat's edge all the way to the stern.

Hal purchased the batalao that was to be their new Ark. He bought also a lighter boat about twenty-five feet long called a montaria. He and Roger preferred to call it a skiff. It was almost as light as a skiff and capable of considerable speed. It also was fitted with a toldo but smaller than the house on the Ark.

With the help of the shipyard proprietor Hal engaged his crew. To man the two boats and to help him and Roger in trapping animals he worked out that he needed six men. Five of his recruits were Indians and the other, whose name was Banco, was a "caboclo" or mixture of Indian and Portuguese.

There would be a third boat, the dugout in which they had descended the Pastaza, but it would simply be towed like a dinghy behind the Ark.

All were highly excited over the prospect of the long jungle voyage as they rowed the Ark and the skiff alongside the raft and proceeded to transfer the animals and the kit from the raft to the boats. It was already getting dark. Hal was anxious to get the work done while the light lasted so that they could sail at dawn.

A crowd collected on the pier to watch and give advice. They were much entertained by the process of hoisting the awkward iguana into the Ark. The great stork, worried by so much company, flew up to the length of his fifty-foot line and circled in the sky. In the meantime the other end of the line was transferred to the Ark and, as the bird descended, it was drawn down gently into its new quarters.

The work was about done when a figure that stood head and shoulders above the rest of the crowd pushed through and came down on the raft.

Hal at once recognized the man. To make sure, he turned on his flashlight. There could be no doubt about it. It was the same brutal face that had leered out of the night at him in Quito.

"Hello," said Hal. "I believe we've met before."

"Oh, that so? Oh yes – for a minute up in Quito. Believe I was trying to find a church."

"I hope you lit your candles and made your prayer."

"All right, buddy, enough of that. I been wanting to see you."

"You took the words right out of my mouth. I've been

wanting to see *you*. I believe you took an interest in this raft when I wasn't around."

"Oh that! Just a case of mistaken identity, mister. We took it for another raft."

"Of course," said Hal. "By the way, I didn't quite get your name."

The stranger laughed. "I ain't much on names. Just call me the boy's best friend." Again he opened his snarling mouth in a laugh, and his teeth were snaggled and discoloured like a crocodile's. Hal at once had a name for him – the name of the big treacherous brute of these waters.

"All right, I'll call you Croc, just to have a handle for you. Now what can I do for you? Besides dumping you overboard."

"Now listen, buddy, I don't want no trouble," said the man christened Croc. "I just want to make a deal with you."

"For Shark Sands?"

The man started with surprise. "I don't know what you're talking about. Now I just wanted to see if you'd like to sell your collection."

"What'll you give for it?"

"A thousand dollars cash."

"It's worth five times that."

"Perhaps," said Croc, a crueller glint coming into his eyes, "but that's what I offer and you'd better take it. If you don't, you'll be kinda sorry. You'd better take it and you'd better do something else. Buy tickets for home."

"And you'd better get off this raft before I throw you off."

Croc's eyes went bloodshot. "You snivelling little rat," he said. "I see I've been too easy with you. All right, if you won't take it the easy way, take it the hard way. I'll be seein' you, buddy."

And he climbed the pier and pushed his way angrily through the crowd.

Roger looked at his brother, wide-eyed. "I have a feeling we're going to see Sunny Boy again before morning."

"It would be just like him to do something during the night to prevent us from leaving," admitted Hal. "Or, if he doesn't do that, at least he will have all night to get ready to chase us down river."

"I know the answer to that one."

"Yes – get a head start. As soon as these people go away we can slip out of here. We can travel all night. Before he can get started we'll be half a day's distance ahead of him."

"But while we're trapping animals, he'll catch up."

"Perhaps so, but there's a chance that we can lose ourselves so that he can't find us."

"What do you mean, 'lose ourselves'?"

"The river is miles wide and full of islands . . . there are dozens of channels between the islands. How will he know which one we have taken?"

"I hope you're right," said Roger devoutly.

Hal called Banco and told him to have the men ready to embark within an hour.

"No, no, *senhor*," said Banco in Portuguese. "We cannot go before morning."

"We are sailing at ten o'clock tonight," said Hal firmly.

"It is dangerous to sail the river at night. No, no, we cannot go."

Hal understood that it was hard for Banco, an older man and well-acquainted with the river, to take orders from a boy. But it was necessary for Banco to learn at the start who was to be boss of this expedition.

Hal took out his wallet. "I'll pay you for this evening's work and we'll go without you."

Banco was thunderstruck. "You can't go without me. You don't know the river."

"I don't know why you think you are so necessary,

Banco," Hal said. "We've come this far without you – we can go on without you."

Banco refused the money. "We'll be ready to sail at ten, *senhor*," he said, a little sullenly.

The animal show being over, the onlookers drifted away to the cafés and plazas. Within an hour the waterfront was deserted. Then a flotilla of three boats slid silently out into the rolling current of the Amazon. The raft was left behind.

"Sunny Boy wanted it," Roger said. "He can have it now."

Banco stood at the helm on the little platform in the stern of the Ark. Up forward, four men stood at the oars. Hal was one of them. The men would have to get used to the idea that the master was going to work right along with them. The dugout was towed behind. Roger was in the montaria with two oarsmen.

The animals were on the Ark inside the toldo, where they would not be worried by the presence of so many strangers on board. Vamp hung upside down in her cage suspended from the roof. The pigmy marmoset clambered from one rafter to another, making nervous chirps. Nosey put his trunk out of the door once in a while, but always retreated, whinnying like a frightened horse. The giant iguana lay on the floor sound asleep, and Stilts maintained his dignity on one foot in a corner.

Charlie, the Jivaro mummy, was the only one allowed to enjoy the fresh air. He was far aloft at the masthead, his black hair waving against the stars.

A tired old last-quarter moon hung in the sky. It was not a bright and cheerful moon, but a moon of mystery and dread. Roger did not like to look at it. Hal was too busy rowing to notice it.

But his blood ran chill as he heard the forest gnashing its teeth. Savage cries from the mouths of hundreds of wild animals combined into one great roar that seemed to be the savage voice of the jungle itself. Most bloodcurdling of all were the ear-splitting howls that one could imagine as coming from a hundred packs of ravenous wolves, or from an army of man-eating lions – but Hal knew that they were merely the night songs of howler monkeys. Although no bigger than a dog, the howler can make more noise than a jaguar. The sound is a deep rumbling roar that would naturally come only from an animal many times as big. A single howler can easily make himself heard at a distance of three miles. The sound is hard for human nerves to endure. It is as if all the agony in the world were being let loose at once. Hal remembered the comment of a naturalist who said that the first time he heard the howler he was so startled he thought all the *tigres* on the Amazon were "engaged in a death struggle".

He could well believe that this was one of the most sullen, morose and savage of the monkeys. If cornered, it would attack viciously and could inflict a severe bite. Its jaws were amazingly powerful. The naturalist Up de Graff had tried to keep one off with the muzzle of his gun – the infuriated creature clamped with his jaws upon the muzzle and bit so hard that he closed the bore.

Hardly less hair-raising were the voices of millions of frogs and toads, booming, moaning, thundering and screeching. They nearly drowned the hoarse croaking of crocodiles, which were evidently numerous along the bank, the whinnying of tapirs, the wild cry of a bird called the horned screamer, the sharp little grunts of peccaries, and many other sounds that were unknown to Hal.

But he had come to know well one sound, the coughing roar of the jaguar. Although it was not very loud, it had the effect of stilling the jungle as if it had been suddenly struck dumb. "Uh-uh-uh-uh-uh!" it went.

The wind freshened. Both boats had been stepped with masts and Hal now ordered up the sails.

Again Banco protested – it was not safe to race down the river in the dark when rocks, sandbars, or half-sunken logs could not be seen. Hal knew that he was quite right, but the desire to put a long distance between him and his pursuer induced him to take the chance.

With both sails and oars at work, the boats flew downstream like scared cats, dodging islands sometimes by only a few feet. Twice the Ark struck a sand bar but managed to struggle across into deep water. Once it struck a log a resounding plunk and the log gave a deep croak and swam away.

The exhausted moon did not give as much light as the stars. The Southern Cross looked frosty in the chill night air. The jungle tumult died down during the middle of the night, then grew again towards dawn. The noise was as good as a clock. When it was at its height, you knew that there was only half an hour left before morning. When the rising sun lit the flowering tops of the trees there was no sound left but the gurgle of the Amazon under the keel and the far cries of a gorgeously coloured flock of roseate spoonbills flying north.

After the sun had risen high enough to reach to the bottom of the leafy gorge the boats were following between two wooded islands, everybody relaxed in its welcome warmth and let the vessels drift while enjoying a breakfast of coffee, mandioca cakes and dried meat.

But the animals, too, were hungry. The island on the

right seemed to be about a mile long. It would be a good place to forage for food for the animal passengers. Hal ordered the flotilla into a quiet cove fringed by majestic Brazil nut trees.

As the boats touched the beach a huge crocodile moved over a few feet to make room, but was too sleepy to swim away. Only its nose and its eyes that bulged like electric bulbs showed above the surface. Its chin rested on the bottom just off the bank.

After a hard night, everyone was glad to rest a while. Most of the men lay on the shore, but Banco and three Indians, afraid of ants and ticks, stretched themselves out in the bottom of the small canoe.

Everyone took a nap. Everyone but Roger.

14
Bucking Bronco Crocodile

Roger forgot that he had sworn off mischief.

The opportunity was too inviting. The crocodile's nose would suit his purpose nicely. It was sharp and pointed, very different from the blunt nose of an alligator. And the crocodile, when it takes off, is as unlike an alligator as a speed boat in comparison with a log raft.

Roger edged over to the painter of the dugout. One end of the line was attached to the bow of the canoe and the other to a log on the shore.

Roger quietly unfastened the line from the log. He made a slip noose in the end of the line. Then he squirmed ever so gently over to the sleepy saurian.

Suddenly leaping into action, he slapped the noose over the crocodile's nose and jumped back out of the way.

The crocodile came to life with a vengeance. It made a lunge at Roger but, missing him, wheeled with a mighty thrash of its powerful tail and plunged out into the bay.

The line came taut with a jerk that shook the sleep out of all four men and set them to yelling like demons. The enraged crocodile yanked the boat this way and that, nearly upsetting it every time he changed his course.

For a time he gave them a free ride, shooting across the bay like a meteor.

Then he turned and rushed at the boat with his great jaws open. They closed with a crunching noise on the gunwale just where Banco's arm had rested an instant before. Splinters flew as the big teeth ground the edge of the boat.

The crocodile changed his tactics. He removed his jaws but brought his heavy tail into action. He swung it like a pile driver against the boat, making it shiver from stem to stern.

Roger by this time had quit laughing. As usual he was having his regrets a little late. Hal and the others had been awakened by the yells. They jumped into the montaria, Roger with them. They set out for the canoe but it shot here and there in such crazy movements that they found themselves going around in circles.

It was still a little funny, Roger thought. How could the men in the canoe be hurt? Banco was reaching over with a knife to cut the line. Then the crocodile would swim away and everyone would think it was a good joke.

Comforting himself with these thoughts, he was horrified to see something happen that he had not thought of. The crocodile dived. Straight down he went in deep water and the canoe followed. The bow dipped and disappeared, the stern rose high in the air. All four men spilled out, the legs and arms going like flails and their yells frightening the birds and monkeys so that the forest broke into a sympathetic din.

Plop! — the four disappeared beneath the surface. Four men in bed with an angry crocodile!

Roger reached for a gun.

"That won't do," Hal cried. "One shot wouldn't kill him. It would only make him worse."

"What'll we do?"

"Cut the painter. He's just frightened. If we can cut that painter perhaps he'll make off."

Hal was about to go overboard but Roger was ahead of him. He knew that this was his job. He dived into the boiling water that was already beginning to show blood. He found the bow of the canoe. With his hunting knife he slashed the line that held the thrashing monster. The crocodile suddenly leaped out of the water like a bucking horse, then dived.

The men righted the canoe and climbed back in. Roger regained the montaria. He had seen the blood in the water and with a heavy heart he looked across at the canoe, expecting to see one of the men badly wounded.

But they appeared to be all right. One of them held a bloody knife. So it was the crocodile that was wounded.

Suddenly there was a new commotion in the bay. Again the crocodile was thrashing about, but this time because it had been attacked by the cannibals of the

Amazon – the ravenous and savage fish called piranhas.

Let a bather, either animal or human, have so much as a scratch on him, and the piranhas, attracted by the blood, are upon him at once. They are only a foot long. With their mouths closed they look as innocent as a perch. When they open their mouths, two semicircles of razor-edged teeth are revealed.

The piranhas are the most feared of all creatures that swim in the Amazon, crocodiles included. They come in shoals, a hundred or a thousand or more at a time. Following up a blood trail, they attack ravenously, stripping all the flesh from the bones in a matter of minutes.

Nor do they always require blood to set them off. More than one canoeist has had his fingers nipped off neatly as he dragged them in the water. A single bite is enough for this operation. The strength of the piranha's jaws is incredible.

A National Geographic Society expedition had found that in catching them it was necessary to use copper wire between the line and the hook. And two strands of the size of wire used for locking turnbuckles on an aeroplane were not enough; three were needed.

The water was churned white by the furious fish. Streaks of deep red appeared in the white.

The Indians in the canoe were jabbering excitedly. They paddled to the scene of conflict. One had a fish spear and proceeded to spear enough food to supply a bountiful fish dinner for everybody. When he had done, more than twenty fish lay in the bottom of the boat. The men kept well out of their way for even a piranha out of water does not become any better tempered.

Close by was a sand bar on which the canoe beached. The fish were spread out on the sand and their heads were chopped off. Roger picked up a head that had been severed from the body for almost a minute and studied the open jaws. He was startled when they snapped shut like a steel spring. He decided to wait until the fish were good and dead before studying them.

An Indian smiled at Roger's surprise. He put the blade of his hunting knife in the mouth of a head that had no body. The jaws snapped shut with such force that the points of the teeth were broken. The Indian took out the knife – on each side the hard steel was nicked in a semicircle by the piranha's teeth.

"At the New York Aquarium," Hal recalled, "a

piranha bit a pair of surgical tweezers made of the very best steel and left nicks in it. They even eat each other. At the aquarium they can't keep more than one in a tank. If they do, the bigger one makes a dinner of the other."

Some of the piranhas had neat slices of meat cut out of their backs. Banco explained that as soon as a piranha is caught on a spear and is helpless to defend himself, all his companions rush upon him. If he isn't drawn out quickly nothing comes up but a skeleton.

"And speaking of skeletons, look at that," Hal said, pointing in the water. The fish had departed, the turmoil had died down, and a long white skeleton like that of a prehistoric monster lay on the bottom.

"That's what they do to our cattle," Banco said. "The cattle are bled by vampire bats during the night; then when they wade into the river the piranhas smell the blood and go at them."

Roger spent the rest of the morning collecting food for his wards. When the noon meal was served all the piranha's sins were forgiven, and Roger's also for the piranha is excellent eating.

Hal even deigned to say, "I don't care if you get into

mischief every day, you young rascal, if it brings us a meal like this!"

But Roger decided within himself that he would get no more fish dinners by tying a canoe to a crocodile.

15
Great Snakes!

Hal kept looking up river for any sign of Croc and the gang of ruffians that he would bring with him.

There was nothing to be seen but an occasional Indian canoe.

Perhaps Croc had not as yet come this far, or perhaps he had already gone by, hidden from view by islands. If he had passed, there was no certainty that he might not return to make a more careful investigation.

Hal was willing to have a fight if necessary, but hoped to avoid it. His business was to make a collection and get out with it, not to fight. The odds would probably be heavily against him. Croc's gang would be made up of armed thugs; Hal's crew were simple boatmen. They had bows and arrows for fishing, and a few blowpipes for catching birds – but no guns.

Besides, Hal did not want any blood on his hands, either his own or that of others. Any killings might lead to arrest, a long stay in jail awaiting trial, and then an ordeal in some Brazilian court. Such affairs sometimes ran on for a year or more. The expedition would be a failure and his father's ruin would be complete.

So Hal resolved to keep out of Croc's way as long as possible. If a gory showdown must come, at least he would not invite it. He would lie low in this cove until dark – then travel again by night.

His men lay on the ground asleep, full of man-eating fish. Hal and Roger followed their example.

So there was no reception committee to welcome the lady who came to call. It was a pity that no one saw her, for she was really a beautiful sight. Her smooth skin was a delicate pale brown ornamented with dark brown spots with light centres. She had a handsome dog-shaped head. She used it to stand on. She was twice as tall as a tall man – in fact the branch around which her handsome red-black-and-yellow tail curled was twelve feet above the ground.

Although tall, she was slender, with a waist measure of no more than twelve inches. Her slim body undulated gracefully as if she were doing a slow dance.

Resting her chin on the ground, she uncoiled her tail from the branch. There she stood for an instant, a muscular column of serpent twelve feet high. Then her body descended to join her head. It did not fall but came down with a smooth balance and poise that an acrobat would have envied.

She raised her head and studied the sleeping forms. How would one of these do for dinner? The boa constrictor, second largest snake in the Americas, is famous for the ability to swallow something three times as big as itself. But the lady in question merely slid over the first Indian, so softly that he felt nothing, then over another and another. Now she had reached Roger. She contemplated him long and thoughtfully. Possibly she decided against him because, although he was not so large as the others, even he would take six weeks to digest.

A sound on the Ark attracted her. Specs, the marmoset, was at the top of the mast playing in Charlie's hair.

The boa slid past Hal's head, crossed the beach, and glided up the gangplank to the deck of the Ark. She stopped to consider the great stork. Now there would be a good meal – but those long bony legs were a nuisance, and there was no nourishment in that big horny beak. Besides, it was sharp and might punch a hole in her skin from the inside – if indeed she could get it inside before it could peck a hole from the outside. The jabiru stork was no mean antagonist. Stilts was eyeing the intruder with stern disapproval and making throaty threats.

The boa turned her attention once more to the juicy little morsel at the masthead. Specs had clambered up the halyards. The boa preferred to use the mast itself as her escalator. It was smooth and slippery but she did not need any projections to climb by. She was not a constrictor for nothing. She could hug her way up.

She spiralled up the mast as swiftly as if it had been lying on the level. Specs did not notice her until her jaws were opening to receive him. He made a wild leap into space and landed on the roof of the toldo.

The boa was confronted by Charlie, who was shaking his head gravely in the afternoon breeze. The movement made him seem very much alive and the boa investigated him with evident curiosity. But she was too fastidious a diner to be satisfied with this shrivelled scrap of human leather. Without nibbling even so much as an ear, she turned and went down, using her own body as a staircase.

She had nearly reached the deck when a little whinny stopped her cold. The young tapir in his gay, yellow-striped coat thrust his enquiring nose from the toldo and then trotted out on deck.

The descending boa, her body still coiled around the mast for half its height, stopped and projected her head. She remained so still that she might have been a bronze statue of herself instead of her living self. Nosey, the little nitwit, wandered straight into the face of danger. His feeble eyes were bent upon the deck on the lookout for food.

When he had come within two feet of her, the boa struck. Her soft, silky neck snapped out as stiff and straight as a ramrod. Her jaws opened and the sharp, incurved teeth closed like a vice on Nosey's nose.

He whinnied to high heaven, at once arousing the sleepers on the beach.

Hal came running, gun in hand. But when he saw the beautiful boa he knew he could not use that gun. He must have this creature for his collection. And yet he could not afford to lose his tapir.

The boa's first act was to lock her jaws upon her prey. Her second was to let her coils come slithering down from the mast and to whip them around the body of the tapir. Her third, if Hal could not act in time, would be to apply the killing pressure, crushing the bones, reducing the flesh to a pulp, and stopping the heart. Then would come the long pull, the animal being slowly drawn down the boa's swollen throat.

Hal fired his gun close to the boa's head, hoping to startle her into releasing her hold.

"I can do better than that," shouted Roger, thinking

his brother had missed. And Banco came tumbling up with a knife.

"Don't hurt the snake," Hal warned. "We want it alive." He jumped into the toldo for some noosing cord.

When he reappeared the situation had changed. A new actor had taken part in the drama. The giant iguana, annoyed by a crack from the whipping tail of the serpent, had sunk its teeth into it. Instantly the deck became a circus for a whirling ball of reptile fury with the innocent little tapir at the centre of it.

Hal and the men stood back. They might as well have tried to stop a tornado. The iguana, looking like a monster of the days before the dawn of civilization, the spines on its back and chin standing out like the hackles of an angry rooster, gripped the snake with its long, sharp claws and held on with its alligator-like teeth. The teeth of the boa had now been transferred from the tapir to her new enemy. But Nosey was so entangled in the coils that he revolved with them, screaming with terror.

Hal looked on in dismay. The two demons would kill each other. The ugly iguana and the lovely boa were both valuable. It was the battle of beauty and the beast. He must not let either win at the expense of the other. But what to do? He had caught snakes before, but never a boa constrictor. What could one do with noosing cord in a mêlée like this?

Another idea came to him and he dropped the cord. He noticed that every time the iguana came out to the full length of the leash that tied him to a log of the craft, the whirling dervishes came to a momentary halt. If he could be there just at that instant and get his fingers on a certain nerve in the snake's neck ... Every snake had such a nerve centre, and it was its tenderest spot, its Achilles' heel.

The next time the line snapped taut Hal's hand flew to the boa's throat, the fingers sinking deeply into the undersurface. He was pulled violently about by the thrashing reptile, but he held on. The Indians were dancing about him, trying to seize some other part of the boa's whirling body.

Then Hal saw that the boa's jaws had relaxed their hold on the iguana. He felt a surge of triumph. He was Tarzan after all.

The feeling changed to one of horror as the boa transferred her full attention to him. Her coils whipped around his body. Roger seized the end of the tail and manfully tried to pull it loose.

"Stand clear!" yelled Hal. One Hunt in trouble was enough. But Roger stuck to his apparently hopeless job.

Hal ground the fingers of both hands into the throat at the back of the snake's head. The open jaws with their gleaming teeth reached back towards his hands. A grip just behind a snake's head is supposed to be safe, but some snakes can almost turn in their skins to get at their captor. Hal was thankful that the boa has no poison, but he was aware that its bite can be painful and sometimes fatal.

"Me kill! Me kill!" screeched Banco, brandishing his knife. But Hal shook his head. He felt he had already won two points, for the iguana and tapir had retreated to safety.

The snake in its violent convulsions got close enough to catch her teeth upon his shirt and tore it from his shoulder. Blood trickled from a scratch.

More serious was the tightening of the coils. He was beginning to lose his breath. With all his strength he tightened his own grip. Then there was a shout of joy from Roger. He was beginning to have some success. The tail came free but whipped about so savagely that Roger, still hanging onto it, danced a fandango. He kept pulling and walked around Hal, unwinding the serpent. The Indians laid hold and helped him. The jaws and the head drooped. Hal relaxed his grip, hoping fervently that he had not gone too far and killed this superb representative of the world of snakes.

The boa went limp and six men had no difficulty in holding her, stretching out her lustrous brown body to full length. The men stood there in a sort of daze.

"Now we've got her, what do we do with her?" came from Roger.

Hal felt bruised and weak. It was as if the wits had been squeezed out of him. Yes, what would they do with the boa now that they had her?

One of the Indians came up with the answer. He pointed to the cabin, or toldo, on the montaria. Sure enough, thought Hal, the Indians were quite accustomed to making a pet of the boa constrictor. In the Indian villages it was common practice to have a boa in the house to keep the place free of rats and mice. This snake had been fighting for its life and had shown its savage nature. But if it were kindly treated it would become tame and even affectionate.

"Just the place for it," said Hal.

Together they carried the weakly squirming boa off the Ark and onto the skiff. They put her into the toldo and closed the door. There she would be apart from the other animals. Perhaps later she would learn to get along with them. If she were kept well-supplied with food, she would have no incentive to gobble up the other passengers. Her first meal was a young peccary brought in by one of the

165

crew. The pig squealed loudly as it was tossed into the toldo. A moment later it still squealed but with a muffled tone, for the squeal was halfway down the boa's throat.

The men opened the door to watch the proceeding. The boa was too fully occupied to pay attention to them. Her head seemed twice as big as before and her throat bulged.

"How can she make her head so large?" puzzled Roger.

"That's because her jaws are not locked together at the back like ours," said Hal. "They're only attached to her skull by a sort of elastic. She can pull her lower jaw away from her upper far enough to take in something a lot bigger than the usual size of her own head. But that's not the most wonderful thing about her. Watch her 'jaw-walking'!"

The boa was inching the peccary in by a curious movement of her lower jaw — or jaws, for there were actually two of them. They worked separately. The right jaw would grip and pull, and the left one would then do the same, the one on the right would release its grip and move forward to grip again, and so on. Thus the victim was "walked" into the mouth and down the throat.

"I see where my job is cut out for me," said Roger ruefully, "getting food every day for that big girl."

"I don't think she'll be much trouble," Hal assured him.

"That meal will last her a week – perhaps two. She'll just lie in a corner and sleep it off. I don't think we even need to keep the door closed. She won't think about escaping until she gets hungry again – and by that time we'll have some more food ready for her."

Roger admired his brother's book knowledge. And it was all to work out exactly as he said except for one unexpected development – something that would provide the expedition with sixty boa constrictors instead of one!

All the rest of day the boa lay asleep in the corner of the toldo. It was possible now to examine her freely. The head could be picked up, the jaws opened, and she could even be turned over on her side.

"Look!" exclaimed Roger. "Feet! She has feet."

Sure enough, just where legs would naturally be if it was natural for a snake to have legs, there were two claws.

"It just shows," Hal said, "that somewhere away back in the ancient history of the boas, they had feet like lizards and other vertebrates. These are the remains of them."

"Why did they lose them, I wonder?"

"Because they became clever enough to walk on their stomachs," Hal guessed. "Think what an advantage it is in the jungle not to have arms and legs to get tangled in the underbrush. A snake can slip through a tangle of vines that would stop anything with legs."

"But none of the snakes we used to catch had these leftover legs."

"No – but I understand all the boa family has them."

"What's the boa family?"

"Oh, there are about forty kinds of boa. The python is one. You'd have to go to Asia to find it. But the biggest of them all, in fact the largest snake in the whole world, you are likely to run into any day here in the Amazon."

"The anaconda?"

Hal nodded. Roger's eyes sparkled. "Are we going to try to get one of them?"

"Yes. But we won't have as easy a time as we had today. Our boa is as gentle as a kitten compared with the anaconda."

"Gentle!" exclaimed Roger, looking at the twelve feet of powerful muscle. "There was a while this afternoon when I thought the kitten was going to swallow a mouse, and you were it."

That night the miracle happened, and one snake became sixty, or perhaps even seventy, no one ever knew exactly how many because it was impossible to tell just how many the big stork swallowed when no one was looking.

The flotilla was sliding down river under a moon even more forlorn than the one the night before. Suddenly, above the bedlam raised by the howler monkeys, frogs and big cats of the forest, came a whoop from Roger. He was in the skiff with two of the Indians. He clutched at his knee, where something was squirming up inside his trousers. Then something dropped from a halyard onto his shoulder and wriggled around his neck.

The two Indians stopped rowing and started yelling. They danced about as if shaking things from their bare feet. Then they scrambled up onto the bow and stood perched there on all fours, chattering like monkeys and looking down with dread into the hold of the boat.

Roger shinned up the mast and looked down. Were his eyes deceived by the weird moonlight, or was the whole inside of the boat crawling?

"What's the matter?" It was Hal's voice. The Ark had pulled alongside and the gunwales of the two boats rubbed. Instantly there could be seen something like little waves or ripples running over the gunwales from the smaller boat to the larger. Then the crew of the Ark joined in the dance.

"Snakes!" yelled Hal. "Are you all right, Roger?"

"They're all over me."

"Have you been bitten?"

"No. They don't seem to bite. But how those little beggars can climb!"

And he slid back to the deck, for he had found that snakes could go up a mast as readily as he.

Hal turned on his flashlight. Snakes everywhere! They were little fellows about a foot long and as thick as a pencil. Hal took one up and pressed its jaws open. He was thankful that there was no sign of poison fangs.

Then it dawned upon him. The big boa had become a mother.

"Whoopee!" he cried. "Now we have enough boas to supply all the zoos in the world."

The other members of the crew were not so happy about it. It was difficult to step anywhere or put a hand to anything without contacting a slithering little form. The youngsters seemed especially fond of pockets. Perhaps they liked the warmth. Hal pulled them out until he was tired and resigned himself to carrying a baby serpent in each pocket.

The Indians were reassured by the evidence of the flashlight. They knew that the little boas were quite harmless — in fact the girls in the villages allowed them to twine through their hair.

Roger was already beginning to worry about having to feed the multitude.

"Perhaps they'll all swim away," he said hopefully.

"No chance," said Hal. "If they were anacondas — yes. But boas don't like the water. They'll probably stay near their mother."

The only other individual on board who was as happy about the snakes as Hal was the big stork. Tonight, tethered out on deck, he thrust his great bill like a shaft of lightning in this direction and that, each time engulfing a snake. His long neck wriggled as they went down. When Hal noticed these goings-on, he quickly put a stop to them by trying the stork's beak shut with a piece of cord.

"That's a job for you," he said to Roger, "to keep Stilts so full of fish that he won't want our babies."

The boats went on their way, raising their sails when a breeze came up shortly after midnight. The jungle was now still. The passage was narrow, between an island and the mainland.

A canoe shot out from the shore into the dim path ahead, and there were shouts in Portuguese. Someone seemed to be calling for help. Hal, though suspicious, could not pass anyone who really needed assistance. He ordered down the sails. The Ark slid up alongside the canoe.

171

"Is this the Hunt outfit?" a voice came from the canoe.

"Yes," said Hal, more suspicious than ever. But what had he to fear from two men in a canoe?

"It's them!" one of the men shouted. And there was an answering shout from the shore and a clattering of oars being made ready in a boat.

"Sails!" called Hal, but before they could be hoisted one of the strangers stood up in the canoe, grasped the gunwale of the Ark with one hand and levelled a revolver with the other.

"The first man who moves will get plugged," he warned.

The men froze in their places as if struck by a sudden paralysis. Roger had been collecting snakes on the deck of the Ark and putting them into a covered basket. He stood with the basket in his arms by the gunwale just above the canoe.

Judging by the sounds from shore there were quite a number of men boarding a boat considerably larger than the canoe in which the two sentinels had been stationed. It was painful to Hal to have to stand helpless while his enemies prepared to attack, but the levelled revolver was very persuasive. It was pointed straight at him.

Roger made a slight movement. The man standing immediately swung the gun to cover him.

"Never mind him," said his companion. "He's only a kid."

The muzzle went back to Hal. Roger felt heartily insulted. So he was only a kid! Not even worth covering with a gun!

He took advantage of the fact that he was not closely watched. He quietly uncovered the basket. A large boat could now be seen putting out from shore, well loaded with men. The oarsmen were being urged on by a ragged-edged voice that was certainly Croc's. Croc's voice reminded you of a stone wall with broken glass on top.

Roger swung the basket and threw the contents upon the two men in the canoe.

16
Bullets at Midnight

A bath of snakes slithered down over the heads of the unwelcome visitors. Bang went the revolver, let off by a nervous trigger finger. The bullet pinged into a tree on the island. The men roared with rage and terror, thrashing about violently, trying to free themselves of the uncanny little crawlers. Who was to know that they were not deadly?

The man standing let go of the gunwale of the Ark in order to have both hands free for his battle with the serpents. He had no sooner done so that he lost his balance and went overboard, capsizing the canoe.

"Hey, I can't swim," blubbered one of the men, but Hal did not tarry to rescue him. The sails were up in a flash and the men bent to the oars. The pursuing boat also ran up a sail.

Hal noticed that the shouted words of the men following were only rarely in Spanish or Portuguese, but mostly in a wharfside English. Croc might have brought the thugs to South America with him or, more likely, he had picked them up in Iquitos. Along the wharves of Iquitos, where ocean liners dock after a voyage of 2,300 miles up the Amazon from the Atlantic, there were always plenty of rough characters from North America or Europe who were quite willing to engage in crime for a consideration. Along with such a gang of willing murderers, Croc doubtless had one or two Indians or caboclos who knew the river. Perhaps one of them was sheeting home the sail, for it seemed to be making the best use of every puff of air.

But the men at the oars could not be river men. Perhaps they were more accustomed to the deck of a cargo steamer than to the rower's post in a montaria. There seemed to be a bank of four oars on each side. Of course they had to work in unison to be successful, but they were continually tangling with each other to the accompaniment of curses that echoed back from the forest wall.

Croc had been forced to pause long enough to pick up the two men dumped from the canoe, right the canoe, and attach the painter to the stern of the larger boat.

"Good boy, Roger!" said Hal, seeing the fruit of his brother's endeavours. Every moment gained might mean the difference between success and failure, life and death.

He felt less cheerful when bullets began to come from the pursuing boat. They zinged by in such a savage hurry that Hal knew they must be coming from powerful rifles of a long enough range to reach them even if they were half a mile away instead of a poor 500 feet.

One struck the stern, one crashed through the toldo, and one crumpled a leg of the helmsman's platform so that it tipped precariously. Banco abandoned the rudder and came tumbling down to safety. The Ark swung off course.

"Get back to the helm," Hal ordered.

Banco replied with a torrent of excited gibberings and huddled down in the shelter of the toldo.

Hal leaped to the platform, grasped the tiller, and brought the Ark back on her course. But a precious moment had been lost.

Bullets smashed around him. What a fool target I must make! he thought. High on the platform, he must be plainly silhouetted against the stars. It could only be a matter of time before he would be hit – unless he could do something to delay Croc's boat.

"Roger!" he called, and Roger came running. "Cut the painter of the dugout."

"What for?"

"Quick! Cut the canoe loose and swing it broadside."

Roger caught the idea. Lay this heavy, hollowed log across the path of Croc's boat. The canoe would be lost, but in a good cause.

He drew in the line until he had his hand on the bow of the canoe. Then he cut the line and gave the log boat a strong push backwards and sidewards. Its forward progress checked, it floated with its port beam towards the oncoming boat.

"That'll stop them for a minute," said Hal jubilantly.

As if in answer a bullet ripped through his trousers barely escaping his hip, and disturbing a boa in his pocket. The snake wriggled, then became quiet again as it snuggled against his warm leg.

The black dugout, he hoped, would blend in with the black of the Ark so that Croc and his men would not be able to see it until it was too late to avoid it.

His guess was nearly correct, but not quite. Croc's boat

was only some ten feet from the floating canoe when it was observed and a hoarsely barked order shifted the course far enough to the right so that the big boat merely grazed the dugout's stern.

A yell of derision came from the boatload of thugs. The yell drowned out a shouted warning in Portuguese. Someone who knew the channel was trying to make himself heard. With all their might, the men at the oars shot their boat straight up onto a sand bar. The keel ground and gritted with a screech, and the sail, still pulling, instantly upset the craft. Some of the occupants rolled out on the bar, some into the water.

Hal's men slackened a little to enjoy the situation.

"Pull!" Hal shouted. "Keep going! If we just keep going, we've got them licked!"

The two boats, with the skiff in the lead and Banco once more at the tiller of the Ark, sped down the dark, winding passage. One or two more shots came from the men on the sand bar, but they went wild. The sound of angry voices died in the distance. Hal breathed again.

But he knew that he could hardly hold his lead. There seemed to be eight or ten men in Croc's gang. Even if they were not very good oarsmen they should be able, with the help of the sail, to propel their light montaria faster than Hal's eight, including himself and Roger, could row two boats, one of them a heavy batalao.

He could not depend upon the sail. The one on the Ark was large and pulled powerfully when the wind was from behind. But both sails were squares and so were useless except with a following wind.

Besides, his job was collecting, and that meant making frequent stops. No, a straight getaway was impossible. The game of hide-and-seek must continue. But it was not easy to hide two large boats made conspicuous by their masts and toldos.

The flotilla swept out of the passage into an expanse of river perhaps five miles wide. It kept getting broader and there was no other island in sight. If dawn found them here they would be as conspicuous as a fly on a windowpane.

The jungle animals were already beginning to announce morning. Gradually the stars dimmed in the east, a cold, grey light crept over the water, small clouds in the sky began to blaze pink, and then up bounced the tropical sun.

Everybody peered back along the course. A speck in the distance was probably Croc's boat. If they could see it, certainly Croc could see the Ark. Unluckily the river was becoming wider and wider. It was now ten miles from shore to shore, and more than ever like a sheet of glass on which it would be impossible to hide.

Hal looked at his map. Ahead there should be a cluster of islands — but beyond them there was another embarrassingly open stretch.

Then he noticed a blue line indicating a passage between what appeared to be the mainland and what really was the mainland. He thanked his stars for a highly detailed map. He looked towards the north shore and could see no passage — but he knew it was there and he changed the course of his little fleet.

"There is nothing there," said Banco. Used to following the main channels, he knew of no such passage.

But it was there, and they found it. The boats were now temporarily cut off from Croc's view by a screen of islands concealing the entrance to the passage. Croc, Hal hoped, would waste time looking for them among the islands and would not discover the little waterway through the jungle.

The passage was narrow and the trees met overhead. Their great white trunks went up two hundred feet before they branched to form a roof. It was like going down the nave of a cathedral — except that no cathedral would be alive with brilliant birds and chattering monkeys. The sails were of no use here, for the breeze was cut off by the forest. However, the surface was glassy smooth, and rowing was easy.

Crocodiles grunted as the waves from the boats struck them. Stilts exchanged remarks with two stately jabirus standing one-legged on the bank.

"Look! A lizard walking on the water!" cried Roger.

Everyone stopped rowing to witness the remarkable sight. The lizard, tail and all, was about three feet long. Its stood on its hind feet and balanced itself with its tail which touched the surface of the water. Its clawed front feet were raised in the air like hands.

"It's a basilisk!" cried Hal.

"It looks savage," Roger said.

"But it isn't. The men who named it thought it must be the ferocious creature of the old stories – you know, a basilisk was supposed to be able to kill a person just by breathing upon him or merely by looking at him. And the way it stands up like man, or a ghost, must have made it seem more weird."

"It must be a ghost," said Roger, beginning to think that his mind was being addled by the mysterious gloom. "How could anything real run on the water?"

The basilisk, in quest of food, ran from one shore to the other, and upstream and downstream, paying no attention to the boats. It went with amazing speed. Whenever it stopped for an instant it began to sink.

"It's body is very light," Hal said. "And see how large and flat its feet are — as broad as lily pads. As long as it keeps going it can stay up. What a sight it would be in a zoo!"

And he set about capturing it. He contrived to get his boats one on either side of the nimble animal. The basilisk was beginning to get worried. An angry red crest rose up on its head, another on its back, and still another on its tail. It looked something like a turkey gobbler with three red banners waving instead of one.

Suddenly leaving the water, it skittered up some twigs which touched the surface, and took refuge on a low branch. Hal made a pass at it with his net on the end of a long pole. But it leaped into the water, disappeared entirely for an instant, then bobbed up like a jack-in-the-box and began to run again.

One of the Indians, a young fellow named Aqua, who was always willing to do more than he was asked to do, made a mighty leap out of the montaria and landed squarely upon the basilisk. They both vanished under the surface. When Aqua came up his arms were empty. The lizard had wriggled free and presently it shot up into the air, reminding one of those reverse motion pictures in which a diver dives out of the water instead of into it.

But now it was really annoyed. With its three crests flaming mad, its jaws open, and sharp claws extended, it lunged straight at Aqua. Even a leaf-eating lizard can be provoked to anger. Aqua made ready to defend himself, but it was Hal who saved him from being badly scratched.

Down came the net, arriving just in time to trap not only the lizard but the head of the Indian. The basilisk, surprised by this new attack, clawed at the net instead of Aqua. The Indian struggled free, and Hal drew the net with its lively contents to the boat.

He lifted the new passenger on board. It was remarkably light for so large an animal. Hal exclaimed over its beautiful colouration – green and brown with dark crossbars and red crests. And what talent! The creature could run equally well on land or on water, was a good swimmer, and could climb trees almost as nimbly as a monkey. Any big zoo would be happy to pay from £100 to £150 for it.

If he could just get it to a zoo! And he gritted his teeth

as he thought of the man who was apparently determined either to steal his collection or destroy it.

The basilisk tried to run off with the net. Two men held the net while Hal ventured to put an arm inside and slip a noose over the animal's head. It was hard to avoid the snapping jaws. Finally the line slipped into place just behind the head crest and forward of the front legs. Hal tied another knot in it to make it fit snugly. No amount of squirming or clawing could dislodge it.

Then he removed the net. The basilisk was now like a dog on a leash, but the leash was thirty feet long. The other end of it was tied to a post of the toldo.

"Why no cage?" Banco asked.

"Would you like to be in a cage? As long as I can, I like to give the animals as much freedom as possible. Besides, if they're not caged, they can help feed themselves."

The basilisk's only idea at the moment was not to feed itself, but to get away. It scooted across the deck and then across ten feet of water to the nearby bank and climbed a tree. Since the boat was moving along, the line at once became well tangled in the brush. The Ark had to be backed up to the shore; Hal untangled the line and drew the protesting lizard on board.

Banco grinned at Hal's embarrassment. "Better let me make a cage," he said.

But Hal stuck to his theories. "When we get a *tigre* you can make a cage for him, but not for a harmless lizard."

He had seen too many animals die in cages. Even in the zoos the trend nowadays was towards providing animals with open parks as similar as possible to their native habitat.

So he tolerated Banco's scorn as his four leashed animals, the tapir, the stork, the iguana and the basilisk, proceeded to wind themselves up with each other. He patiently unwound them as often as necessary.

The woodland waterway was eight miles long. It came out, according to the map, at the junction of the Napo and Amazon rivers.

Whether they were being followed down the passage, Hal could not tell. But he had a new plan for eluding his pursuer. When the end of the channel was reached, he directed his little fleet not out into the great waters of the Amazon, where it would again be clearly visible, but to the left, up the Napo.

Soon the bends in this river concealed the boats from any voyagers on the Amazon. Hal selected a quiet cove and made ready to spend the rest of the day there.

This time no gangplanks were run out. The baby boas would have used them to escape to shore. The boats were moored some twenty feet out and the men waded to the beach.

Roger was the first ashore, and therefore the first to stumble into trouble.

17
Wrestling Match

Roger gaped. He rubbed his eyes. This couldn't be true. There just couldn't be any such animal.

It stood up like a bear on its hind legs. It looked like a bear as far up as its neck. From there on it looked like nothing else in heaven or on earth. Its head was all snout. There was no mouth, no jaws, nothing but a small hole at the end of the snout. And out of this hole came chain lightning.

The creature had huge muscular forearms like a gorilla's and great curved claws four inches long. With these it was tearing open a huge anthill that stood as high as a man. As the ants swarmed out, a red, fiery, lightning-like tongue nearly two feet long darted in and out so fast that it was impossible to follow it.

Hal arrived on the scene. "A giant ant bear!" he shouted. "We must get that."

Roger marvelled. "I didn't know an anteater grew that big."

"There are different varieties. This is the largest. What a find!"

"Well, if it's only an anteater," said Roger scornfully, "I can grab it for you. You got the last thing — the basilisk. Let me nab this one." And he started forward.

"Look out! It's dangerous."

"Dangerous? How could it be, with only a tongue? It hasn't a tooth in its head."

"But its claws—"

"I'll grab it from behind."

The ant bear, in spite of very poor eyesight, realized that something was wrong. It brought its front paws down to the ground and lumbered off, slowly and awkwardly, with its front feet turned in. Behind it came the most fantastic tail Roger had ever seen — an immense brush two feet thick and several feet long. The entire weird outfit from snout tip to tail tip easily measured seven feet.

Roger came down with a flying tackle on the ant bear's back and locked his arms around its chest. He expected now to carry it out to the Ark, and that would be that.

He was more than a little surprised when the supposedly timid anteater reared up on its hind feet and scratched his hands so badly with its claws that he had to let go. He jumped out of the way of the slashing claws.

The anteater, still on its hind feet, sparred like a pugilist, advancing upon Roger and striking out with one arm and then the other. The red tongue darted like the tongue of a snake.

Hal was worried, but he knew that Roger would not thank him for interfering. He was ready to give the bear a smashing blow on the head with the stock of his gun if the situation became too critical.

"Lay off," Roger panted. "This is my bear."

Retreating, he stumbled against a log, and went over backwards. Instantly the hairy giant was upon him. The embrace that Roger had given it was now returned with interest. Like the bear of northern climes, this one knew how to hug. Hal remembered that it was said to be able to crush the life out a puma in this fashion.

But Roger was not done. He struggled to his feet, bringing the bear erect with him. No stranger wrestling match had ever been seen. Roger got hold of the long snout and made as if he were trying to unscrew it. The gigantic tail switched and thrashed about, whipping him on one side of the face and then on the other, or getting in front of his eyes so that he could not see what he was doing. But he could always feel that tremendous and increasing pressure.

He tripped the beast and sent it hurtling on its back, but it did not relax its hold. The wrestlers were up again in a flash. Roger tried lifting his opponent clear of the ground, but it hung on just the same. The sticky red tongue slapped into Roger's face. It seemed to be covered with mucilage. Roger let the bear take full honours in that kind of attack. His own tongue was dry and tight against the roof of his mouth.

He could not stand this hugging much longer. He violently twisted the snout – that was the easiest thing to get hold of. If a boxer didn't like to get punched in the nose, why shouldn't an ant bear's nose be sensitive too?

Suddenly the bushes parted and a new gladiator entered the arena. Another big ant bear came to the aid of its companion.

Two against one. It wasn't fair. Hal levelled his gun at the newcomer. But it was so close to Roger that he did not dare shoot.

Aqua leaped in with a knife – if one could call his thirty-inch-long machete a mere knife. It was practically a sword, and a murderous-looking one at that.

Up came the ant bear on to its hind feet. It stood fully six feet high. Aqua was five inches shorter.

The other bear had chosen to wrestle with Roger. This

one preferred to fight a duel with deadly weapons. Its great gorilla-arms flailed out at the Indian. Each arm ended in three sabres, four inches long, and razor-sharp. They were keen enough and powerful enough to tear open anthills made of baked clay almost as hard as cement. So firm were these hills that the downpours of the rainy season had no effect upon them, and it was difficult to dent them with a hammer or a hatchet. Yet an anteater sometimes kept slashing at a ten or twelve-foot-high hill until it had brought it completely to the ground. It would attack a log so firm on the outside that an axe would raise clean chips – and would hack its way through to the rotten heart filled with termites.

It was quite capable of making ribbons out of Aqua, if it could just get at him. But Aqua fenced skilfully. He parried every thrust with his machete. Whenever there was a chance he lunged at the creature's body. He could seldom reach it. His knife was long but the bear's arms were longer. Once when he came too close he received a deep slash on his chest. The blood welled out and Hal started to his rescue, but Aqua waved him back. He, like Roger, wanted to win his fight alone.

Aqua had one advantage over his opponent. The bear was fast with his arms, but slow on his feet. Aqua was fast all over. But, on the other hand, the bear fought with six blades, Aqua with one.

Aqua feinted a jump to the right, but, as the bear was turning, he leaped to the left and closed in on the animal's flank. Before it could turn, he swung his machete with all his strength and cut cleanly through the neck. The long pointed head dropped off. The body dropped to the ground, but the muscles still jerked. Blood poured out. One of the men came running with a bottle – the blood would make a most acceptable dinner for Vamp.

But Roger and his giant had not suspended operations to watch the duel.

"Hold tight!" yelled Hal. "Don't let him slash you."

Roger clung close so that the bear could not swing at him with those vicious daggers. But he felt the claws sinking into his back. And the embrace of the beast was crushing him. He could not stand this sort of thing much longer.

Then he had an idea. He wrestled the bear out to the water's edge. Perhaps anteaters hated water. He was wrong in that – the anteater is an excellent swimmer. Nevertheless, Roger was on the right track. The bear did not mind being dragged out into the bay – but when Roger dipped its pointed nose under the surface and held it there, it showed signs of discouragement.

Now it fought to free itself, but Roger hung on. In its struggles it pulled Roger from his footing and he suddenly found himself on the bottom of the bay with the bear on top of him. He was now getting a dose of the medicine that he had prescribed for his antagonist. The question was simple: Which one of them could last longer without breathing?

The bear gave in first and rose to take breath. He did not get it, for Roger took care that the long proboscis he was still clutching should not come above the surface of the water. The bear's muscles relaxed.

"Don't drown it," came Hal's warning.

Roger dragged the now inert body of the anteater out of the water and dropped it on the deck of the Ark.

The captive opened its weak eyes, flicked its red tongue, and made a few feeble passes with its claws. Hal noosed a heavy line about its body to make a sort of harness before and behind the front legs, and made fast the other end. The bear now had the liberty of a very short leash.

"If he behaves himself, we'll give him more rope later," Hal said.

The wounds of the gladiators were treated. Roger felt like a collapsed balloon and stretched himself out on the beach.

"Guess you'll have to do the foraging today," he said to Hal. "And I don't envy you the job of getting enough ants for that bear!"

Hal was poring over one of his manuals. "It says here that they live for years in the zoos on chopped meat and raw eggs. They don't have to have ants." His brow knitted as he read on. "Gosh, if I'd known this I wouldn't have let you play with that bear. They really *are* bad. They've killed plenty of Indians. Here's an account of one that even killed a jaguar – sank its claws into the heart. And a hunting dog is apt to be ripped open from stem to stern before it can get near enough to bite."

"Then perhaps it will get tough with our other animals?"

"No. They say it's very peaceable – provided it's let alone."

"Well, believe me, I'll let it alone from now on," moaned Roger.

The Indians carved up the dead beast and ant bear steaks were featured on the luncheon menu.

The meat was tough, wiry, and as sour as vinegar. Roger took one bite and no more. Hal made a brave business of finishing his portion, but his face was screwed up into a knot with distaste.

"Believe I'd almost rather have plain ant without bear," he said.

195

18
Go West, Young Man

"Fire!" exclaimed Hal.

His fleet was once more sailing down the Amazon.

As it rounded a point, a red reflection came across the water from a blaze on shore.

"An Indian village burning up," Roger guessed.

"No Indian village," Banco said. "Young man from Rio. He made a farm here. Perhaps attacked by Indians."

"Steer for the shore," Hal ordered.

Banco did not move the tiller. "Indians may be there still. We would all be killed."

"We could help him put out the fire," Hal insisted. "Make for shore."

Banco stubbornly held his course. Hal mounted the platform and forced over the tiller. The caboclo went down to the deck, muttering.

Both boats were moored a few feet from shore, for Hal was ever mindful of his cargo of little boas that would escape if the vessels were allowed to touch the bank. The men leaped ashore.

Hal and Roger each took the precaution to carry a rifle, and the Indians were armed with bows and arrows and spears.

Banco made a show of trying the edge of his long knife but he lagged behind when the men climbed the bank. He had no stomach for a fight. When no one seemed to be noticing, he turned back towards the boats.

But Hal had been watching him. He was not quite ready to believe that Banco would cut loose and sail away, leaving them to whatever fate was awaiting them. But he was taking no chances.

"Up in front!" he ordered sharply. "Quick, get up in front. You are going to lead us."

Banco grumbled and growled, but he went forward with the willing Aqua and stayed there for a while at least.

As soon as they topped the bank they could see the fire plainly. A frame farmhouse was ablaze. There were no Indians to be seen. A lone man was vainly trying to douse the flames with buckets of water from the well.

Hal broke into a run. He took care to see that Banco ran also, encouraging him by pressing the muzzle of his revolver between his shoulders. So stimulated, Banco developed remarkable speed.

The man looked round and, seeing armed men rushing at him, he had every reason to think that he was about to be attacked. He clapped his hand to where his revolver should have been – but there was no revolver.

"Have you got some more buckets," cried Hal, not thinking to try to say it in Portuguese.

The man looked mightily relieved. "Over in the shed," he answered in English.

Hal and his crew dashed to the shed and found an assortment of buckets, pails, and cans.

Then to the well. It was equipped with an endless chain to which were attached six tubs. As the windlass was turned they came up full and each man in turn filled his vessel, ran to toss the water on the fire, and came back for more.

The roof of the little house was of corrugated iron. That may not be beautiful, especially when it has been rusted by Amazon rains, but it has the advantage of being fireproof. The blaze in the walls was quickly put out by the relay of fire fighters. The young farmer went inside the somewhat blackened interior and lit a lamp. Then he slumped to the floor.

Hal and Roger carried him to his bunk. He lay there as limp as a rag, with eyes closed. Hal went over him to see if he was wounded. Aqua took a towel from the wall, ran out to soak it in water, and returned to put it over the prostrate man's forehead.

Hal admired the strong, clean-cut, and intelligent features of the young farmer. Then the eyes fluttered and opened. A wan smile passed over the pale face. The lips moved and he spoke just one word: "Thanks."

Roger came with a glass of water and they held the man's head as he drank. The eyes of their patient roved about the room and they followed his gaze. Everything was at sixes and sevens, empty boxes on the floor, cupboards open and stripped of their contents. It was plain that the man had been robbed. The place had been thoroughly looted. Nothing of value remained, only scraps and fragments. Blood was spattered over papers and floor. Hal picked up a purse. It was empty.

"You must have had a real fight," Hal said, looking at the smashed chairs and the bloodstains.

The farmer nodded. "A real fight," he said faintly.

"Do you live here all alone?"

Another nod.

"Isn't that dangerous – in Indian country?"

"They weren't Indians."

"Not Indians! Then who . . . ?" He guessed the truth. Croc's gang. "What language did they speak?"

"English, mostly. They asked me if I had seen boats with animals go by. I said no. They wanted food. There were eight or ten of them to feed, and I gave them all I could spare. Still they demanded more. They helped themselves, took all my supplies, put them in their boats. When I objected, the big fellow knocked me down."

"The one with a face like a vampire bat's?"

"That's right. How did you know?"

"I've met him. In fact, he's chasing us down river. We're the ones with the animals. I hope that's his blood."

"I'm afraid not. I went for my guns but they had already stolen them. I got a knife. When the big fellow saw it he slipped behind the others and let one of them take it. The fellow I cut swore he'd get revenge. He fired the house. They took me out and held me off until the fire was too strong for me to stop it. Then they let me go and went off to their boats. By the way they laughed, they must have thought it was very funny."

"How does it happen that you speak English? You're not English?"

"No, Brazilian. My name is Pero Sousa. I learned English in school in Rio."

"I've heard it's the most beautiful city in the world," said Hal. "Why did you ever leave it?"

The young pioneer smiled and lay quiet a moment before he answered. "There were posters on the walls in Rio. They said just what used to be said in North America – 'Go West, Young Man'. Only they said it in Portuguese. Our government wanted us to develop this back country. So I came. Perhaps I was foolish." He lay quiet again, eyes closed.

Then he opened his eyes and a light burned in them. "No, I wasn't foolish," he said fiercely. "Not unless Columbus was foolish when he went west to discover the New World. Not unless the Pilgrims were foolish when they went west to land on Plymouth Rock. Not unless Americans were foolish when they went west to build the United States." He raised himself on his elbow and fixed his eyes intently upon Hal. "Think what a chance there is here for young fellows like you and me. This is the world's last great frontier. A lot of it hasn't even been explored. It's rich in minerals. It has the biggest forests of fine woods on earth. It has the world's greatest river to carry all of its products to the sea. This Amazon valley could feed the world. But not unless it has men – plenty of men. Now there's less than one man to the square mile. Think of that! In the United States there are forty-three to the square mile, and nobody considers that country crowded. We need men – not just Brazilians, but men from your country and everywhere. There are fortunes waiting here for men who are willing to work."

"You had better rest just now," Hal advised.

"Fortunes!" Pero repeated. "But the most important thing is not the money we can make here. The most important thing is peace in the world. And why don't we have peace? Because there is too much suffering and hunger. If the Amazon is brought into production it can relieve that suffering and hunger."

"I know," said Hal. "But don't you think you'd better relax now and get some sleep?"

Pero smiled and settled back on his pillow. "This must all sound like hot air to you. But tomorrow morning I'll take you around the farm. You won't believe it until you see it — what this soil will do."

Hal looked about at the fire-ruined walls, the smashed furniture, the gun racks without guns, the looted drawers and boxes, the empty purse.

"Don't you realize that you have been wiped out?" he said. "You have no guns, no clothes, no supplies, no money to buy seeds or farm machinery. I can see you have a good education. You would do well in the city. Why don't you go back to Rio? We'll take you down-river. If this happened once it will happen again. There are plenty of other gangs like that one. Besides, there are always the Indians. One man can't do anything against the jungle. Go with us tomorrow morning."

But Pero only smiled that gentle, tired smile of his. "Thank you, my friend. But I'll stay here. In the morning I'll show you why."

And, in the morning, Hal understood why. Pero could not show him the pigs, for they had been stolen; nor the cattle, for they had been slaughtered and the meat taken away to feed Croc's gang. But the thieves had not been able to take away the vegetable gardens in which beans, rice, corn, lettuce, cucumbers, radishes, and carrots flourished. Hal was astonished.

"But I understood that the soil was so leached by the rains that nothing much would grow."

"That's the story," laughed Pero. "But you can judge for yourself whether it is true. The only trouble we have is that things grow *too* fast. We have to be all the time fighting back the jungle, and fighting down the weeds. Things grow as if by magic. A bamboo shoot will grow a foot in a night. I'm not joking. Seed corn that would take two or three weeks to bud in the United States, buds here in three days. And look at the size of those oranges."

Hal gazed at a young tree loaded with fruit as big as footballs.

"They can't be oranges! No oranges ever grew to that size."

"They are oranges. In California they call it the Washington navel, but they got it from Brazil. It grows only one-third as large in California."

There were young mango trees, avocado trees, cocoa trees, breadfruit trees, banana plants, all heavily loaded with fruit. There was a tract of good pasture land covered with fresh green elephant grass. In the woods within the borders of Pero's property were fine hardwoods, mahogany, cedar, rubber, towering skyscrapers of trees loaded with Brazil nuts and cream nuts, and huge, wide-spreading fig and garlic trees. There were trees valuable for their oils, much in demand in the industrial north. Pero was right. The world needed Amazonia. Men who dared to bring its riches to mankind were performing a great service.

"Just to show you how important all this is," Pero said, "the United Nations is taking a hand in it now. They've raised millions of dollars from all the nations that are interested in what the Amazon has to give them. They've organized what they call the Amazon Institute – and they're sending dozens of experts in mining, forestry, agriculture, and everything else, down into this country to map out its possibilities. Some of them were here. They liked my farm."

Hal put out his hand and gripped Pero's.

"I don't blame you for sticking. Good luck!"

But when Hal and his crew sailed away they were short one revolver and the precious .270 Winchester rifle. They hung on the gun racks in Pero's cabin. He would discover them there in due time. He would also find a box of ammunition for the guns, some clothing, and, in one of the pockets, his own purse, not empty.

But Pero had given Hal more than Hal had given him
— a new determination to win in spite of both man and
jungle.

19
Tiger Comes to Call

Days passed with no sign of Croc. He continued pursuing, not knowing that what he pursued was behind him. Sooner or later he would realize the truth and would lie in ambush for the arrival of the Ark. Hal kept a constant lookout.

He kept taking on new passengers, most of them small: a gorgeous scarlet ibis, a roseate spoonbill, a golden conure, a cock of the rock, and a curassow that soon became a pet.

But Hal was dissatisfied.

"These small things are all right. But we've just got to get an anaconda. And a tiger."

He took his problem to Aqua. He had come to rely more and more upon the faithful young Indian. During the long hours on deck Aqua had been teaching the two boys the *lingua geral*, which means general language. Each Amazon tribe has its own language, but there is also a general language known to Indians throughout the great Amazon basin. Any explorer should be acquainted with it, since many Indians did not speak Portuguese, and almost none of them knew English.

"I think you will get *el tigre* soon," Aqua said. "We are coming now into tiger country."

"I can never get this quite straight," complained Roger. "Is it a tiger or a jaguar?"

"Jaguar is the literary name for it," Hal admitted. "But you won't find anybody down here calling it that. South Americans call it a tiger and since it's a South American beast I suppose they have a right to name it. I'll call it a tiger too. No matter what we call it, I want one."

"You say it's South American," Roger objected. "But we heard of one in Arizona."

"Yes, and there are plenty of them in Mexico. But they're different. They're small. They seldom weigh over fifteen stone – these run up to thirty. The Mexican animals are dark coloured – these are a bright yellow with black marks. Of course the mark isn't a stripe; it's a sort of broken ring. The Mexican variety will run away from trouble if it can. These down here don't hesitate to charge. And they're very fierce and strong. I've just been reading here what Sasha Siemel says about them. He says that a South American tiger can kill an African lion."

"Isn't he the fellow they call the 'Tiger Man'?"

"Yes. The big cattle ranches employ him. The tigers are hard on cattle. One ranch loses three thousand cattle a year to the tigers. Siemel fights with a spear. He thinks it's more reliable than a gun — because it takes a lot of shots to kill a tiger. Even when you shoot a tiger through the heart it may continue its charge and kill you before it dies."

"I'll enjoy seeing you tackle a tiger with a spear," Roger grinned.

"I'm afraid you won't have that pleasure. That's an old Indian custom — I'll leave that to Aqua. But I hope it won't be necessary; we want to capture one alive, not dead."

Tigers were certainly becoming more common. Their roars at night were more frequent. The terrifying thing about the roar of a tiger was that it seemed to be very close at hand even if the animal were two or three miles away. The roar began with a series of coughs that came faster and faster and louder and louder until they turned into a thunder that seemed to shake the woods — certainly it shook the nerves of anybody listening. Then the cry died away and ended in a few grunting growls. When it was all finished the air seemed to be still vibrating.

You could tell, roughly, how near the animal was by the grunts at the end of its roar.

"If you cannot hear those grunts, he is far away," Aqua

said. "If you can hear them, watch out – he is close!"

The roar, with its rise and fall, had the eerie effect of a siren. It was hard to sleep through it. Travelling was now done mostly by day and hammocks were slung on shore at night. A camp fire was kept burning all night. Hal was never quite sure of this fire – did it keep animals off, or attract them? Perhaps it frightened the more timid ones. But one night he looked from his hammock to see a great yellow-and-black head not twenty feet from him. The tiger did not see him but was gazing with evident curiosity at the fire, its big yellow eyes gleaming in the light. Presently the animal lay down full length, for all the world like a cat by the hearth. Its enormous jaws opened in a gigantic cat yawn.

Hal was quite unprepared for this visit. He had no cage ready, no net, and his men were asleep, some on shore and some on the montaria. Those who did not mind having baby boas crawling over them were on the boat.

If he called to the men, the animal would be alarmed. His gun lay beside him but he could not bring himself to use it. He did not want to kill the superb beast. On the other hand, he did not care to go to sleep within twenty feet of a tiger – and the tiger seemed to have no notion of leaving.

One of the Indians rose to put more wood on the fire. The tiger sat up on its haunches and watched the proceeding with interest. Hal hardly dared breathe. Softly he took up his Savage and aimed, but did not fire. One bullet would only change a placid cat into a raging devil.

At least he hoped the cat was placid. He told himself that animals, even the most savage ones, rarely attack man unless they are cornered or wounded. But he knew that this did not quite hold true of the jaguar. There were too many cases of man-eating on record. Lumber-jacks and rubber gatherers were frequently killed by tigers. A sailor escaped but left an arm behind him. Three padres were caught in a church; two were killed and the other got away. In the Buenos Aires zoo was a tiger that had taken three lives. Then there was the Argentine scientist whose camp was visited every night by a tiger that had taken a fancy to the dried beef; when it was hung out of reach the disappointed tiger attacked the man himself, smashing his skull with one crunch of his jaw.

There were dozens of other cases Hal had read of, but he could not remember them now. He did recall only too clearly one reported by the naturalist Azara: six men went to sleep around a camp fire; in the morning four of them awoke and found the bodies of the other two that had been dragged some distance into the jungle and half devoured.

The Indian came around between the fire and the tiger. Hal's finger fondled the trigger. He could feel the cold sweat on his forehead. The tiger stretched out its nose, as if sniffing. Would this brown, two-legged creature make a good meal or not? But it did not move.

Suddenly, back in the brush, there came the high whinny of a tapir. Instantly the tiger's great head swung around in that direction. It rose and padded off without a sound.

Presently out of the jungle came a terrific noise – the shrill screeching of the tapir and the thundering roar of the forest king.

Everyone in camp woke up with a start.

Roger said with an unsteady voice, "Gee, I'm glad we have a fire. That really does keep them off."

Hal did not choose to worry his brother by telling him what he had seen. In five minutes Roger was asleep again. But Hal kept watch the rest of the night.

In the morning he found the tracks. Each footprint was as big as a soup plate. It was almost perfectly round. The spaces between the toes were even and there was no sign of claws – the jaguar keeps them drawn well back as he walks.

There was nothing about the print to suggest that it had been made by a savage beast. It was as soft and smooth as if someone had pressed a velvet pad into the dirt. Hal remarked about this to Aqua.

"The *tigre's* paw *is* soft," Aqua said, "but strong! Just one blow from it will kill an ox."

With Aqua's help, Hal and Roger followed the trail back into the jungle. They came at last to the spot where the struggle between the tapir and tiger had evidently taken place. The grass was trampled, earth torn up, and underbrush broken. But there was no carcass of a dead tapir.

Hal was disappointed. He had hoped to capture the tiger here. When the big cat kills a large animal it usually eats what it can, leaves the carcass for some hours, and returns to eat again. The wily hunter will be there with his gun or his cage at the time of the second visit.

But this time the tiger had been more wily than the hunter.

"Look at the path," cried Roger. "There must be Indians."

"No Indians," said Aqua. "The tiger made this path."

"But it's as wide as three tigers."

"He was dragging the tapir."

Hal stared. It was hard to believe. Out of the trampled arena led what was almost a road, three or four feet wide, with every bit of underbrush flattened as if a steam roller had passed over it.

"How could a jaguar drag a tapir?" he marvelled. "It's as heavy as a cow."

There was no doubt about it. The largest of South American wild animals had been dragged through virgin forest that even a man with a machete and no burden would have had trouble in penetrating.

They followed the trail. In some places it was more of a tunnel than a path since the tiger did not stand more than three feet high. They stooped and scrambled through.

At any moment they expected to come upon the carcass, and perhaps the tiger. But the trail went on for more than a mile. Then it came out on the bank of the Amazon. It continued to the water's edge. And that was all.

Hal looked across the river. It was several miles wide. His respect for the jaguar grew.

"I didn't know it could swim," said Roger.

"Better than you can. The jaguar loves the water. Perhaps his wife and kids live on the other side and he wanted them to share his meal. But think of swimming all that distance pulling something twice as heavy as himself!" But

Hal remembered the account in one of his manuals of a jaguar that killed a horse and swam with it across the river; and the report by the famous Brazilian, General Rondon, of a horse that was dragged a mile through heavy brush to a water hole where the jaguar might enjoy drinks with his meal.

The cleverness of the animal was almost equal to its strength. It could have gone straight to the river past the camp – but it took a roundabout route to avoid any risk of losing its prize.

On the way back to camp, Aqua showed the boys a strange sight – a tigers' manicure parlour. It was a large tree. At a height of about six or seven feet above the ground were deep scars and scratches made by the claws of jaguars.

This was the way, Aqua explained, that they sharpened their claws. They behaved just like house cats. Standing on their hind feet up against the tree, they dragged their claws repeatedly through the bark. Where their breasts rubbed the tree, it was worn smooth.

20
Tigers Take No Nonsense

Tiger country it was. That became clear during the day's voyage.

Roger was up ahead in the skiff. Suddenly he signalled his two men to stop rowing. He pointed to a cove. Hal stopped his oarsmen and the Ark drifted up alongside the skiff.

On the log projecting out over the cove was a large jaguar. His great head was turned the other way and he did not see the silent boats. He was busy fishing.

He was using his tail as bait — or, rather, as a lure. He would tap the surface of the water lightly with his tail. Insects or fruit dropping upon the surface would make a similar sound. The fish would come up to investigate.

Suddenly the tiger made a quick thrust into the water with his paw and came up with a fish in his claws. He popped it into his mouth and ate it with relish. He looked lazily about and saw the boats. He got up slowly, too dignified to run, and walked solemnly into the forest.

Aqua was grinning. "Very smart tiger," he said proudly, as if he owned it.

Roger was not willing to believe what he had seen. "Do you think he was really using his tail to attract the fish? What does your book say, professor?"

Hal was, as usual, deep in a manual. "Well, here's something pretty wonderful. And it's by a naturalist you can trust – Wallace. Listen to this:

"'The jaguar, say the Indians, is the most cunning animal in the forest: he can imitate the voice of almost every bird and animal so exactly as to draw them towards him: he fishes in the rivers, lashing the water with his tail to imitate falling fruit, and, when the fish approach, hooks them up with his claws. He catches and eats turtles, and I have myself found the unbroken shells which he has completely cleaned out with his paws: he even attacks the cowfish in its own element, and an eye-witness assured me that he had watched one dragging out of the water this bulky animal, weighing as much as a large ox.'"

"Wow!" commented Roger. "And you think you're going to catch anything as strong and as smart as that! You're crazy."

Banco became interested. "Does the *senhor* wish to catch a *tigre*?"

"That's what I'm aiming to do," said Hal. He hoped

that Banco, who had been a pretty sour customer during the trip so far, was now going to offer to help him. It was a vain hope.

"You cannot capture a *tigre*," said Banco.

"Why not?"

"It needs twenty or thirty men. We are only seven men, and a boy."

"But the 'tiger man' kills a tiger single-handed."

"He kills it. He doesn't take it alive. That's different."

Hal had to admit the truth of this. But he was all the more determined to take home a tiger.

He cut short the day's journey at noon and ordered a landing. After eating, the men were set at work building a cage. When Banco objected, Hal said, "Banco, we're going to stay right here until we get a tiger — no matter if it takes a month."

To make the cage not only strong but light, stout bamboos were lashed together with green, wiry lianas. A door was built at one end. The cage was kept small enough so that the animal could not get leverage to break it. It was about four feet wide, four feet deep, and ten feet long.

Nearby Hal found a trail to the shore where animals were accustomed to come down to drink. He looked eagerly for tiger tracks, but had to call Aqua. The Indian found them, and they were big enough to satisfy the most ambitious collector.

Hal and his men began to dig a pit. The Indians were willing to work, but Banco sat on the sidelines muttering to himself. The pit was made six feet deep and about as wide. It was squarely in the middle of the trail.

Then the men, under Hal's direction, cut some poles and laid them across the hole. Hal laid the heavy loop of a lasso on the poles. Then he climbed the great fig tree that overhung the pit and tied the other end of the lasso to a branch, making the rope between the branch and the loop fairly taut.

Then the poles and the loop were covered with leaves and dirt so that the pit was no longer visible.

The cage was brought up and placed nearby, but out of sight among the bushes.

The idea was that the tiger should fall through the loop which would tighten around him as he dropped into the pit. Then he would be drawn out and dragged into the cage. Banco snorted sarcastically.

"This you cannot do," he said.

They retired to camp and waited. It was just getting dark when Hal heard a commotion in the direction of the trail. He stole through the woods to the pit.

But he was due for disappointment. The pit was occupied, but not by a tiger. The great blunderbuss of the woods, the tapir, had fallen into it. Hal already had a tapir and did not want to take on another. Space in the boats was too precious.

It was a two-hour job to haul out the heavy beast, cut it free, repair the pit, cover it, and reset the lasso.

Then back to camp for another wait. But Hal was less hopeful than before.

"Aqua," he said, "we don't want all the animals in the jungle falling into that pit. We want a tiger."

"Then let us call one," said Aqua.

He went to his pack of belongings and brought out a steer horn. Hal followed him to the trail at the point where it came out on the riverbank.

Aqua put his lips to the horn and a sound that certainly did not sound like Aqua's voice came from it. It was exactly the voice of a tiger, beginning with a few deep coughs, rising to a fiendish roar, and dying down to low, slow grunts. It was so that moose were called in the north woods – but how different the call!

They listened. The small animals of the forest had been paralysed into silence by the roar. But there was no answering tiger call.

"Guess we're in for a night of it," Hal said.

All night, at intervals, Aqua made his call. It was not until just before dawn that there was a distant coughing answer. A faint grey was lightening the black river, but the darkness inside the jungle was still complete.

Aqua called again. Again the answer. Each time it was closer. Now they could hear the low grunts at the end of the call. That meant that the animal was not more than a mile away.

Closer and closer it came until it seemed that the beast must be just beside them in the bushes. Then a roar was cut off in the middle – and when it came again it had a new note. It was not the voice of one coming to meet a friend, but of one who had been tricked and trapped by an enemy. There was so much savage rage in it that the icicles prickled up and down Hal's back.

"He's in the pit!" he said.

They ran to the pit, where they were joined by the others from the camp. The pit was like a huge pot furiously boiling with something that showed yellow and black in the dawn. Everyone shouted with joy except Banco, and even he seemed sourly impressed.

The rope hung straight and taut from the tree, and the branch to which it was fastened was shaking violently. Evidently the tiger was well caught in the noose.

Now the little matter of getting him into the cage! Hal looked at the wildly churning mass of muscle with dismay and the ear-splitting roars of the beast unsteadied his nerves. This whirling demon was certainly in no mood to walk into a cage.

Hal had the cage brought up to the edge of the pit, and the door opened. He climbed the tree and untied the end of the line. He came down, passed the rope in through the door and out at the back between the slats. Now, if everybody would pull, the tiger might be drawn up out of the pit and into the cage.

It was an excellent theory. Tigers had been caught that way. But he reckoned without Banco. That gentleman, instead of pulling with the rest, sat under the tree and made sneering remarks.

The tiger, furiously trying to climb out of the pit, was helped by the men pulling on the rope. Now he was up to the door of the cage. He could not see the men back in the bushes, but Banco was plainly visible.

The big cat's eyes blazed, and with a terrific roar he lunged at Banco. The rope scorched through the men's hands and was pulled free. Banco let out the most piercing yell of his life and scrambled up the tree.

If he had had time to think he might have acted

differently. It was the worst thing he could do. The jaguar, expert tree climber, came up after him.

"Shoot him! Shoot him!" screamed Banco. Hal's Savage was in his hand but he did not raise it.

Higher and higher went Banco. Perhaps he thought that if he got up into branches that were weak enough, the heavy jaguar could not follow. This might have worked if he had not run into a wasps' nest.

An angry buzzing stopped him. His fingers had broken the nest and the residents came out a hundred strong to see who their visitor was. The welkin rang with his cries of distress as he was stung in dozens of places at once, on face, hands, legs, and through his thin shirt. The tiger was coming on, sinking his claws deep into the bark, and moving with the terrifying grace and beauty of a great snake.

Not that Banco saw any grace and beauty in it! He looked down into two eyes like headlights and open jaws lined with sharp teeth. The tiger was no longer tearing the sky apart with his roar. He was growling softly and deeply as if enjoying the prospect of such an easy meal.

Hal was ashamed of himself for viewing this spectacle with so much satisfaction. But he could not idly leave

Banco to the wasps and the tiger. He caught the end of the rope and lashed it around a branch so that the animal could not go any higher.

Banco did not know that this had been done and expected to be seized and devoured at any instant. Hal was content to let him live in terror a moment longer. Perhaps it would be good for him. Banco thrashed furiously at the wasps, only exciting them to more stinging. Slapping and striking, he lost his grip and slipped down towards the waiting jaws. He caught himself just in time.

Hal's heart popped into his mouth. Perhaps he was carrying this game just a little too far.

He called the men, loosened the rope, and they all laid to and began to draw the beast down the tree. The cage was brought to the foot of the tree and the rope was once more passed in through the door and out the back.

"All together!" cried Hal. "Pull!"

They pulled with a will, and the rope broke.

Instantly Hal was shinning up the tree. He had dropped his rifle, but his revolver was in its holster. He knew what he had to do. Kill the tiger before it killed Banco. Banco was screaming hysterically. The tiger was inching steadily upwards. They were so close together that Hal had not dare to fire from the ground for fear of hitting the man instead of the beast.

The tiger, with a savage growl, made a lunge at one of Banco's feet, missing it by inches. Banco pulled it out of reach, retreated farther into the wasps' nest, and shrieked to high heaven.

The tiger was making ready for another lunge when Hal brought the butt of his revolver cracking down on one of the animal's hind feet. It had the desired effect. The beast forgot Banco and turned to face his new tormentor. His head was now out of line with the cringing form above and Hal fired.

He didn't wait to see if the bullet had found its mark. The earsplitting roar told him that it had. He slid down the tree so fast that he ruined a pair of shorts. He was certain the tiger would follow – and it did.

He had no sooner reached the ground than the tiger leaped from a branch fifteen feet up and came whizzing down to land on the spot where his enemy had just been. But Hal had made a quick jump to one side. He fired again. He missed. His hand shook, the revolver wobbled. He fired again and again. He realized now that Roger was firing with the Savage. The tiger rolled over, got up, wheezed blood, bellowed hoarsely, and came on again.

Hal felt sick and numb. Everything was a blur, the tiger, the men, the woods, all whirling madly. He tried to get hold of himself. He fired straight into open jaws that were spewing blood over him.

Then he was conscious that someone else was in the fight. Aqua was there with his spear. It was the famous old Indian way of fighting, the way that had been adopted also by the "tiger man". But the spear had two blades instead of one. It was something like a two-tined fork.

The tiger was already shot through and through. Yet he charged again with a coughing roar that filled the air with red spray. No man could have stopped that express train. Aqua did not try to stop it with his own strength. He let the earth beneath him do the work. As the weapon pierced the tiger's chest, Aqua pressed the other end of the spear into the earth, thus letting it take the force of the blow.

The tiger was stopped dead in his tracks. Aqua lunged forward with the spear, trying to push the animal over onto its back. But the tiger swerved, shook itself loose from the spear, and came on again with a roar, making a leap at Aqua's throat.

Hal and Roger kept firing. The king of the jungle was being steadily shredded to bits but he fought on. Again Aqua plunged the spear into his chest and the other end into the ground. The spear bent like a bow but it stopped the charge. The tiger staggered weakly. While it was off balance, Aqua heaved with all his might.

Over went the animal onto its back. But all its four paws were towards Aqua, clawing the air. The Indian side-stepped to get behind the beast's head, still pinning the body firmly to the ground.

Once behind the head, he could work more safely. He was out of reach of the powerful legs which shot out in all directions as the animal furiously tried to wrench loose.

Aqua see-sawed the spear back and forth, pressing it farther and farther in, piercing the heart. Hal emptied the rest of his revolver into the great head. There was a wild struggle that tore up the earth and brush for yards around. But the roars were becoming weaker. The big feet swiped the air with less force. The powerful beast went limp and lay still, blood flowing from the heart.

The two boys and Aqua had no sense of victory. This was a battle they had lost, not won. They still had to take a tiger alive.

21
Tiger by the Tail

The crew ate the dead jaguar, in spite of the fact that the taste of it was not very agreeable. Indians believe that eating a brave animal makes you brave. Hal waited a day and a night for another jaguar to come along the trail, but none came.

"All right," he said, "if they won't come to us, we'll go to them."

He and Roger and three of the Indians struck back up the trail into the jungle following tiger tracks. The spoor, marked plainly in the soft ground, led them finally to a low ridge in the side of which was a cave. The tracks disappeared within the cave.

Hal approached the entrance cautiously. He drew his revolver but hoped fervently that he would not have to use it. One death struggle with a tiger was enough.

He peered into the darkness. He could see nothing and could hear no growling, nor even breathing. But there was a strong animal smell. Perhaps the cave was deep and the tigers were far back.

The men carried a net of strong manila rope, and this Hal place over the mouth of the cave. It completely covered the opening. The four corners were staked to the face of the bank – but very lightly, so that the plunging of the tiger into the net would tear them loose. Hal made fast a heavy line to each corner. At a distance of ten feet these four lines were joined and braided to form a single heavy cable which went up over a branch of a tree and down again within reach.

If a tiger ran out into the net the four corners would come loose and close in on the animal. Then everybody would haul on the rope which passed over the branch and down to the net. Shut inside the net, the tiger would be lifted clear of the ground. There the beast would be quite helpless. After it had spent its fury, it might be manoeuvred into the cage, net and all. The door would be locked. Then the net could be eased off and pulled out through the slats.

Hal had read all about it in a book.

Four men were placed on duty at the end of the rope. Every four hours they were relieved by another squad. The two times when something was most likely to happen were sunset and sunrise. It is then that the jaguar prefers to go out to drink at the river or a waterhole.

All day Hal and his men were on watch and after the sun had gone down the suspense was hard to bear. Nothing happened. The net flapped idly in the evening breeze. The jungle animals started their evening chorus, but there was no sound from the cave. Hal was disgusted.

"I will show you another way to get *el tigre*," Aqua said. "Come down to the river."

Hal was glad of a change. He left four men on duty at the cave and went with Aqua. They waded out to the skiff. Taking up the anchor, they rowed the boat well away from the camp. Aqua rummaged in the toldo and brought out another net.

Then he produced his steer horn and put it to his mouth. Hal thought that no tiger could have made a better tiger call.

"On nights like this when the river is smooth," Aqua said, "*el tigre* likes to go swimming. A *tigre* in the water is easier to catch. He is too busy swimming to fight."

Again and again he called. Hours passed. Hal was cold and sleepy. He had always supposed that hunting a tiger would be the most exciting sport in the world. He was bored. He longed for his hammock and a heavy blanket.

"I think he is coming," whispered Aqua, and Hal shook off his drowsiness. Somewhere between the boat and shore, grunts sounded of a sort that could not come from a crocodile. Aqua called again. There were more grunts or coughs, half-smothered by water.

Then Hal could see something swimming. He kept perfectly still. Now he could make out a tiger's head, but it was small. His hands tightened on the net as he made ready to throw it.

The swimmer paused, as if uncertain. Aqua called again, very softly. It must have been good tiger language, for the tiger came on.

Hal was not sleepy now. He tingled all over with excitement. He realized too late that he had not given enough thought to his plan of campaign. He had placed too much confidence in Aqua.

Suppose they caught the tiger in the net – then what?

He had no time to figure this out, for the tiger was now beside the boat. The top of its head showed above the water, also the tip of its tail. By reaching out, Hal could grab that tail.

He had a sudden inspiration. His arm shot out and he seized the tail.

"Row, Aqua, row!" He heaved upwards on the tail, sinking the tiger's head in the water. "Row like mad!"

Aqua leaped to the oars and pulled. Hal braced himself and held on. A gurgling roar sounded from somewhere under the surface. The tiger was dragged along by its tail. It thrashed about savagely but could not get its head forward nor its front paws up. Much of the time the head was under water. The animal was, in fact, rapidly being drowned. It stopped struggling. Now it was a dead weight. Hal called to Aqua and they lifted it into the boat. This was not too hard, for it was a small animal – weighing not more than eleven stone.

They laid it on the net. Even in the dim light they could see that it was a beautiful animal, a real prize. Hal hoped they had not thoroughly drowned it. He cautiously felt for the heart – it was still beating.

He wondered if he should apply first aid. It wasn't necessary to decide this question, for the tiger stirred.

Hal jumped to his feet. "Quick! Close the net!"

They brought up the edges of the net and lashed them together. It was none too soon. The tiger was growling now and striking out feebly. She would spend the next few hours trying to get out of that net, but she was as safe as a kitten in a bag. They fastened the net to the mast.

"That'll do until morning. Then we'll make a cage for her."

Hal was not satisfied. The little tiger was valuable, but he still wondered what was in that cave.

When nothing came out at dawn, he decided to go in and investigate.

He held a revolver in one hand and a pole in the other. Near the end of the pole, but not at the very end, was strapped a flashlight.

If he found a tiger he hoped to confuse it with the light, prod it with the pole, and make it run out into the net.

He walked slowly back into the cave, playing the light before him. The cave was deep and twisted off to the left. As he came to the turn he heard a low growl in the darkness. He began to wish he had stayed out in the sun.

He moved the light beam here and there but could see nothing, nothing but two bright spots. Then he realized that the two spots were eyes. Another growl made him feel cold.

In vain he tried to pick up the rest of the body with his light. Surely he could see a brilliant yellow skin with black marks. But there seemed to be nothing but those two burning eyes. Again came a challenging growl.

Hal reminded himself that a wild animal usually does not attack unless it is cornered. He must be careful not to corner this one.

He went far over to the right wall so that the beast might escape along the left side. The cave was wide and there was plenty of room for it to get by without coming near him. Then it would rush out and they would have a big tiger in the net.

He knew it must be big by the deepness of the growl and the distance between the eyes. But he was greatly puzzled because he could not see the rest of the animal. There appeared to be nothing around those eyes but black cave.

He waited, but the tiger did not move. Hal crept forward, close to the wall. He still hoped the beast would not insist upon being prodded.

It was no use. The closer he came the louder the growls, but the beast did not stir.

Or was it stirring? Yes, the eyes moved now. They were moving towards Hal. This would not do. Hal shouted, but the eyes came on.

He fired into the wall to alarm the beast. He could have fired between those eyes but he was still resolved to get this one alive. He crowded against the wall. Why didn't the animal run past him and out into the net?

The end of the pole struck something hard between the two eyes. Hal could see it now – it was the face of a black jaguar. His heart leaped. This was the greatest animal treasure of the Amazon jungle. Black jaguars were as rare as hen's teeth. He could not think of a zoo that had one – or of a zoo that did not want one and would not pay handsomely for it.

No matter what happened he would not use his revolver. He slipped it into the holster. He put both hands to the pole and gave the tiger a manful jab on the left cheek, hoping to divert the beast to the other side of the cave and out into the net.

He might as well have jabbed a rock. The tiger took two more prods without seeming to notice them. Then he swiped the pole with one big paw. The pole was smashed into splinters against the wall and the light went out. A deafening roar filled the cave. Hal turned and fled.

Around the turn he went with the vengeful beast close behind. No Olympic runner could have beat Hal Hunt then. With a flying leap he plunged into the middle of the net. He prayed that he would hit it with enough force so that it would break loose and not bounce him back into the savage jaws.

The net did break loose. Then men at the rope had heard the roar and they were ready. As something, they did not know what, struck the net they hauled.

Up went the net like a bag with Hal inside. The astonishment of the crew who had bagged a man instead of a tiger can be imagined. They were speechless with surprise, and then they laughed. How they laughed! The tiger halted at the mouth of the cave and then retreated into the darkness.

Hal would have given anything to be on the other side of the globe at that moment. The men's hilarious laughter made him feel pretty small. It didn't help much that his own brother, Roger, laughed more loudly than anyone else. He rolled on the ground, kicking the dust, and screaming with joy. When he could speak again he said, "Oh boy! Won't this be a good one to tell when we get home!"

Dangling from his branch, Hal said gruffly, "Let me down."

The men were too merry to be careful. Paying out the rope, they neglected to hold tight – it slipped through their hands and down Hal came, in a heap. This did not help to soothe his pride. He pushed the net away from him and got up. He stepped out of the net with great dignity.

"Ho, ho! The great tiger man!" chortled Roger.

Hal looked about at the laughing faces. His nerves had been badly shaken but he was getting control of them now. After all, it must have been pretty funny. He grinned.

"Too bad you didn't have a camera, Roger," he said. "That was sure one for the book."

But his thoughts were grimly fixed upon the magnificent creature in the cave. He was going to get that tiger!

22
Black Beauty

It was a council of war.

Hal, Roger and Aqua were trying to decide how to capture the black beauty. They were not getting very far.

"We've got to nab it," Hal said. "It's the last word in tigers. Even a Bengal tiger isn't worth as much. But the net idea won't work with this big fellow. He's too wise."

Aqua was stirring up some bird-lime. He had made it from the juice of the breadfruit tree. It was more sticky than thick paste or flypaper.

The Indians used it to catch birds. They would smear some of it on the limb of a tree where birds were in the habit of alighting. A bird that came in contact with it could not get away. When it beat its wings, they too would be caught. It stayed there until the hunter came for it.

Aqua had been using the method to catch birds for some of the hungry animal passengers.

Suddenly he paused and stared at Hal. An idea was breaking in the Indian's head. He pointed at the bird-lime.

"This will catch the tiger," he said.

Hal laughed incredulously. "It's good for birds — and perhaps monkeys — but you might as well try to stop a tiger with a bottle of mucilage."

"This will catch the tiger," Aqua repeated. "All our people use it."

He called in some of the other Indians as witnesses. They nodded when he explained his idea and told stories of how they or their friends had captured the big cats with bird-lime.

Hal thought he was being kidded. Perhaps the men had not forgotten what a ridiculous figure he had cut hanging from a branch in a bag. They thought they could make a fool of him. And yet Aqua had always been respectful before this.

Well, if it was a bluff, he would call their bluff.

"Okay," he said. "You and the boys can go ahead and catch Black Beauty with bird-lime."

Aqua leaped up and talked excitedly with the other Indians. They went to gather more of the sticky substance. They took it to the tiger trail at a point a few hundred feet from the cave.

They took the net that had trapped Hal and laid it on the trail. They covered it carefully with leaves so that it

241

was not visible. They spread great quantities of bird-lime on the leaves. Then they scattered more leaves on top.

"Now all we have to do is to wait," said Aqua.

Wait, wait! Animal collecting was nine-tenths waiting. Hal hung his hammock in the woods within easy earshot of the trail. Aqua slept nearby. They alternated watches through the night. They heard no tiger.

In the morning they crept to the trail and found an agouti caught in the lime. The agouti is a two-foot-long rodent.

Hal was disgusted. He was about to tear the animal loose when Aqua said, "Leave it there. It will draw *el tigre*."

A low growl made them wheel about.

At the mouth of the cave stood the most splendid of jaguars. He was black as night, sleek, long and powerful. His yellow eyes blazed. His savage black face parted in a snarl that showed gleaming white teeth. He looked quite capable of carrying out the reputation that the black jaguar has among the Indians of being the most ferocious of the cat tribe.

He had been cooped up in the cave long enough. He was about to go to the river for a drink of water and anyone who got in his way would be unlucky.

Hal was about to take to the woods, but Aqua said, "No. He might come after us. That would take him away from the lime."

Instead of going into the woods, Aqua ran down the trail, Hal following. Now the snare was between them and the tiger. They were, like the agouti, tiger bait.

The huge black beast came padding down the trail. It was wonderful that an animal so heavy could move with such smooth grace. Within that glossy pelt there must be nearly thirty stone of bone and muscle.

Hal, remembering his encounter with the black monster in the cave, did not welcome another interview. He was distinctly uncomfortable. What if Aqua's plan did not work? Suppose the beast merely walked through the bird-lime and came on? Was this powerful brute going to be stopped by a little stickum?

The tiger's pace quickened. He broke from a walk into a well-oiled run, his glossy shoulders moving like pistons. If Hal had not been scared to death he would have admitted that it was the loveliest movement of muscle he had ever seen.

Why didn't the beast pay attention to the agouti? He seemed to look straight past it at the two men. Hal felt very foolish, standing in plain view, waiting for a tiger to

pounce upon him. And he hated that low, vicious growl. He would rather hear the beast roar. But the tiger was not wasting his breath on roars.

He was now almost up to the snare. Suddenly the agouti caught his eye and he stopped dead. He crouched to the ground. For a full minute he lay there, little black ripples moving along his muscles as he tensed them.

Then he sprang.

What a leap it was, all of a dozen feet. In mid air he roared, and his roar shook the forest. He came down like a black avalanche upon the helpless agouti and seized it by the neck.

But instantly he let it go. His attention was attracted by the stuff under his feet.

Now, thought Hal, we shall see if bird-lime can hold a tiger. No, Aqua was wrong. The tiger was now lifting one foot. It was covered with white. Then he raised another paw and looked at it with surprise.

Hal had had enough of this. "See!" he cried. "It isn't holding him. Come on. Let's get out of here."

But Aqua put a hand on his arm. "Wait. You do not understand. Watch."

The tiger was trying to lick the stuff off his paw. It did not come off. He bit at it savagely. He got it smeared over

245

his face. He tried to rub it from his face. He only succeeded in plastering it over his eyes. He lay down in order to get the use of his four paws. Now the strange stuff was all over one flank. He tried to get it off and only succeeded in making matters worse.

Now Hal understood. His grandmother had told him of the old custom of putting butter on a cat's paws to keep it busy until it became used to a new home. The cat was so fully occupied that it had no time to worry about anything else.

And so the tiger was not worrying now about the agouti or the two men. He was a cat with only one idea – to get rid of that gum. Cats of all kinds like to be clean.

Roger and some of the Indians arrived in time to see the strange spectacle. The tiger saw them out of smeared eyes and gave them a few growls; then went back to licking and biting at his fur. He sat up on his haunches and began washing his face with his paws, exactly like a house cat.

"I think we can take him now," Aqua said.

He had the Indians bring up the cage. He passed the net rope through the front door and out between the slats. Then he drew gently on the rope, making tension on the four lines that went to the four corners of the net. The other men laid hold to help him.

"Slowly, slowly," he said.

The far edge of the net draped itself lightly over the tiger. The beast was drawn inch by inch into the cage. His own struggles helped. Every time he moved any part of his body in the right direction the net was tightened so that he could not move back. At last both the net and its sticky contents were inside the cage. The door was locked. The prisoner took his mind off his work long enough to make a few thrusts at the bars, then went back to his task.

"He'll be doing that for a week," Aqua said. "He won't stop until he gets every bit of it off his fur."

The tiger paid no heed to anything but bird-lime as the cage, set on two long poles, was carried down to the river. The Ark was brought up and the cage was hoisted on the deck and set in the toldo. The agouti, which one of the Indians had cut loose from the net, was served for dinner.

Hal beamed with delight and went around congratulating everybody, even Banco. He owed a special debt of gratitude to Aqua. This exploit had crowned the expedition with success.

Well, almost. He still wanted an anaconda. And he still had to escape Croc, get the collection down river, and on board a steamer for home.

But he was so happy that nothing seemed very difficult now.

23
Giant Anaconda

You can't strike a match on an anaconda. It was Hal who made this remarkable scientific discovery.

He had voyaged two hundred miles further down the Amazon. His collection had been increased by one upside-down sloth, one well-plated armadillo, and one small, graceful Amazon deer.

They were moored in a little bay where they had spent the night. It was not a clean-cut bay with sand beaches, but marshy, the sort of place, Aqua said, where anacondas might abound.

In the morning Hal went aboard the Ark to see how the animals were faring.

He found the wood ibis gone. Only a few feathers remained. Its cage had been smashed. The bird could not have done that. Only something heavy and powerful could have accomplished it.

He looked about at his other animals to see if any of them had a guilty look in its eye. The giant iguana had its eyes closed and lay basking in the morning sun. It was quite capable of such a deed, but its leash was too short.

The basilisk was a strict vegetarian. It was out at the end of its line for a morning run on the water. The great stork had only one eye open and it didn't look guilty. The jabiru stork enjoys mice, frogs and fish, but is not enough of a cannibal to consume other birds and would certainly draw the line at eating its own cousin, the wood ibis.

The way the cage was smashed suggested that the boa constrictor had done it, but this was impossible since the boa was in the other boat, sound asleep, still digesting her pig.

Hal gave it up. The vampire bat was chirping her call for breakfast.

Hal set about preparing Vamp's meal. He got out a bottle of defibrinated blood – that is, blood from which the fibrin had been removed by whipping. The fibrin is what makes blood clot. Vamp would not accept clotted blood. But it was too much of a job to obtain a fresh animal for her daily. The blood of a single capybara would feed her for three days – if it could be kept fresh. The blood in the bottle was three days old, but still liquid thin.

But it was cold. Hal poured a cupful of it into a pan which he placed in the fireplace in the corner of the toldo. He arranged some shavings and sticks under the pan. Now to start a fire.

He had the habit of striking his matches on a post of the toldo. But this time the first match failed to light. He tried it again and again, then threw it away. He tried more matches, but they did no better.

In the half-dark of the toldo he thought the post looked peculiar, but his eyes were still blinded by the outside sunlight and he could not see very well. He tried another post. His match lit at once.

When the fire was blazing he looked up at the post that had failed him. Then he backed off from it, his nerves doing a dance. A huge snake was coiled around the post. He had been trying to light matches on its scales.

He thought at first that it was his boa, escaped from the montaria – but then he saw that it had none of the boa's colour and grace, and it was three times as big.

He realized with a jolt that he was looking at the anaconda, the world's largest snake. The royal python of India was sometimes longer, but more slender and lighter in weight.

He could not estimate the length of this serpent because of the way it was coiled around the post, but he could see that it was more than a foot thick. At one place there was a special bulge – perhaps that was Hal's wood ibis!

The body was an evil-looking dark green and the head

251

was black. The eyes were fixed upon Hal, who could not move, he was so fascinated. He thought of the stories told by Indians of how the anaconda is supposed to be able to hypnotize man or beast with those terrible eyes. Hal did not believe such tales. But he felt numb and it was only with an effort that he walked out of the toldo. He glanced back uneasily but the snake had not moved.

Hal tried to shout to his friends on shore. His voice would not come. It was not until he got ashore that he could command himself.

"An anaconda!" he said breathlessly. "There's an anaconda in the toldo."

The men were greatly excited by the news. "Let's catch it," Roger said.

"All right, but how? You don't just go up and throw your arms around an anaconda."

Hal sat down on a log and tried to think. If they noosed the snake in the toldo it would thrash about, tear the toldo to bits, kill the other animals, and quite possibly sink the Ark.

Aqua had helped him before. Hal turned to Aqua now. But the Indian had no suggestion.

"We never take it," he said. "The Indians all fear it."

"But you make a pet of the boa constrictor."

Aqua smiled. "The boa is our friend; the anaconda is our worst enemy. The 'deer swallower' is full of devils."

Hal noticed that Aqua had used one of the Indian names for the anaconda – the deer swallower. It gave him an idea.

"Perhaps we can use the deer to attract the snake to the shore. Once we get it ashore we might be able to make it fast with lines."

The idea was passed on to the men. Not one of them was willing, not even Aqua, to go aboard the vessel of which the anaconda was now master and try to use the deer as snake bait. Each man was afraid that he might prove to be more attractive bait than the deer.

The plan bounced back upon Hal.

"All right, I'll go," he said, and gingerly walked out the gang-plank which had been laid from the Ark to the bank – for there was no danger now of the baby boas swimming ashore since they had become too large to roam freely and had been confined in a cage.

Before leading forth the little deer to its fate he would make sure that his prize was still there. He glanced inside the toldo. The fire was sputtering weakly and a few rays of sunshine came in through the holes in the thatch roof.

But the post was no longer draped with serpent. The

anaconda was gone. It would be hard to say whether Hal was disappointed or relieved. There was a large hole low down in the reed wall. The snake must have gone that way, then slid over the gunwale into the water.

As Hal stood, wondering what to do next, something like an earthquake seemed to shake the heavy boat. Hal staggered out of the toldo expecting to see that some large waves were running in from the Amazon. There were no waves. He looked ashore and could see no sign of earthquake. Anyhow, this was not a land of earthquakes.

While he stood there puzzling over the mystery, suddenly the two tons of boat beneath him heaved up bodily and rolled against the bank. Hal lost his footing and went sprawling on the slanting deck. He crawled ashore into a circle of excited men. The boat was on an even keel once more but the water boiled around it.

"It is the anaconda!" Aqua exclaimed. "There must be a nest of them here."

Banco was ordering up the men. "We will leave here at once. The anacondas are very bad snakes. They are evil spirits." He played on the superstitions of the Indians. All sorts of devils were supposed to make their home within this malevolent serpent.

Hal stopped Banco with "We will not leave here without

trying to get an anaconda. But first we'd better get a cage ready for him. It really ought to be a bath-tub." And he told Roger the story of a New York artist who borrowed a fifteen-foot anaconda for the purpose of painting a picture of it. Seeking advice from the great snake man, Raymond L. Ditmars of the New York Zoo, he constructed in his Greenwich Village apartment a pen about twelve feet long containing a wooden bathtub five feet long, thirty inches high, and a yard wide. This worked very well – until a leak from the tub soaked through to the apartment below and the tenants there complained to the landlord. That worthy objected to having a serpent as a tenant and both the snake and the artist had to move.

So a bathtub was constructed for the hoped-for prize. But a bathtub could not be made out of sticks, and there were no boards to be had.

Aqua solved the problem.

"We will make a woodskin," he said.

"Good," said Hal. "Take over the men and do it."

Hal had seen many woodskins on the river. A "woodskin" is a boat made out of the skin of a tree, that is, the bark. A boat would do nicely as a bathtub. And a woodskin could be made far more quickly than a dugout.

The men located a large purpleheart tree. They cut a

line through the bark around the base and, erecting a scaffolding of poles, cut another line twenty feet up. Then they made a vertical cut, and began to pry the bark off with wedges. When it was free, they had a sheet of bark twenty feet long and about ten feet wide.

The ends were laced shut with lianas and "cocked up" with tough vines and "bush ropes", and the crack was made watertight with latex from the rubber tree.

Now it would keep water out like any good boat; or keep water in like any good bathtub.

It was necessary to construct a bathroom – that is, a cage to contain the bathtub and its occupant.

The men worked rapidly but it was the next day before the curious tub-in-a-cage was finished and set in the last available space on the deck of the Ark and Hal could begin to think of getting a tenant for it. Hal was determined that this time no anaconda should find him unprepared. He planned his campaign carefully. He strung a line from the mast of the Ark to a tree some forty feet within the beach. He tethered the deer to this line near the water's edge.

Then he prepared three nooses, one for the anaconda's head and the other two for its tail. The cage was placed in readiness.

Now all that was needed was the anaconda.

The men hid in the bushes and watched. It was the old game of waiting once more. The day wore on. The deer nibbled at the grasses that fringed the beach. It was a beautiful animal, small compared with its Canadian cousin, with a glossy tan coat, large brown eyes and fine antlers. Hal hoped he would not have to sacrifice it.

After three hours of watchful waiting, Hal's desire for action got the better of him. Were there really any anacondas in the bay? Was there actually an anaconda nest as Aqua had supposed? And what did an anaconda nest look like? That was something that he as a scientific observer ought to know.

He slipped out of the bushes, across the beach, and into the water. The bottom dropped off steeply. With a few powerful strokes he was under the surface, looking for trouble. It was hard to see because of the cloudiness of the water. He first made sure that there were none of the man-eating piranhas about. Then he looked for anything that might be described as an anaconda nest.

It was something like going through the jungle, because long reeds grew up from the bottom. They were slimy and disagreeable to the touch. Sunken logs lay about in crisscross fashion and under them there might be a refuge for small animals but certainly not for a family of the largest snakes in the world.

He came to the top to breathe and went down again. Now he studied the steep bank that fell off from the beach. Suddenly he found himself at the mouth of a submarine cave running back into the bank.

If he wanted any proof that this was the nest he got it at once. Two small snakes not more than five feet long came out of the cave and swam off through the reeds. Then the large terrible-looking head of an adult anaconda protruded from the cave. It moved towards Hal.

Hal lost his appetite for investigation and rose to the surface. He could already imagine those great jaws closing on one of his legs. Then he would be drawn down inside that black cave and devoured at leisure. He went through agonies of fear during the instant that it took him to scramble up on the beach.

"What did you see?" whispered Roger.

"Anacondas at home," said Hall. "You're sitting right on top of their house. There's a big cave running back beneath you."

"But how could they live in a cave under water? Don't they have to breathe air?"

"Perhaps the roof of the cave is above the water line," guessed Hal.

Another long wait. Roger dropped off to sleep.

Hal grew tired of watching the ripples that lapped near the feet of the deer, so at first he did not notice something that had broken the surface of the bay. Then he saw it, and it was moving. It was something like the periscope of a submarine. He realized that it was the nose of an anaconda. This snake has adapted itself to life in the water by developing a nose, not in the usual place, but high up on its head so that it may breathe while keeping the head submerged.

Now and then a ripple gave a glimpse of the eyes. They were placed well out so that they could look not only up and forward, but down, a feat of which land snakes were not capable. They were placed so far apart that it was plain the head that carried them must be very large.

And the great head was coming straight towards the deer. Behind the head the water was disturbed far back, showing that under the surface there must be a huge propeller at work – a propeller perhaps twenty or thirty feet long, who could say? The longer the better, thought Hal.

Hastily he slipped through the bushes to the tree and

laid hold of the line. He was glad to see that an Indian who had been posted on the Ark at the other end of the line was awake.

The moving head arrived at the beach. It slid out of the water with the chin resting on the sand. The deer saw it and would have taken to its heels if the line had not held it. The terrified animal struggled violently, its hooves tearing up the sand and flinging pebbles into the snake's jaws.

Hal began to pull on the line and the Indian at the other end paid out accordingly. The deer was drawn slowly towards the tree. The snake followed. Every time the anaconda seemed about to strike, Hal drew the deer out of its reach. Hal himself was concealed behind the tree. The other men were hidden in the bushes.

When the deer reached the tree the anaconda was six feet behind and coming fast.

"All right, boys, go to it!" shouted Hal.

He leaped out with the head noose. The men closed in on both sides with the tail ropes.

When the snake saw Hal it did not retreat but raised its head menacingly. The slightest mistake now would be serious. The snake was about to strike. Before it could do so it must be noosed by the head and the tail.

Hal shot forward straight for the villainous head and the jaws that were already parting to make a meal of him. He slapped the noose over the bulging head and drew it tight on the slender neck.

The other end of the noose rope ran into and through the cage in the usual fashion. The end of it had been made fast to a tree. With the tail held firm, so that it would not lash about, it should be possible to draw the snake inch by inch into the cage.

But it was not to be so easy. The men with the tail ropes became excited and confused. They managed to get only one of the nooses in place. As the snake plunged forward towards Hal, whipping its tail, this rope was jerked out of the Indian's hands.

Banco and two Indians were knocked flat by the thrashing tail. Aqua boldly leaped in with the other noose. The tail suddenly whirled forward and encircled him. He fought wildly to free himself. The loop of serpent holding him moved up the snake's body so that the tail was again free. It continued to flail about.

Roger, trying to catch the flying tail rope, was given a swinging swipe on the side of the head that knocked him unconscious.

Not held by the tail as it should have been, the snake

was advancing upon Hal. Backing up, he tripped and fell. In the second or two that he lay there he lived a lifetime. All the tales he had heard of anacondas devouring cattle, of a horse found in an anaconda's stomach, of men who had lost their lives to this fearless serpent, flashed through his mind. His time had come.

But while his brain was taking the long way around, his body was working like chain lightning. He jerked himself out of the way of the striking head and leaped to his feet.

He saw with horror that Aqua was already lifeless, blood spouting from his mouth and ears, his body tossing limply about. Hal's hand went for his revolver but it had been thrown out of its holster when he fell.

The snake was turning its jaws towards Aqua. Hal leaped for the snake's head and buried his thumbs in its eyes. He held on grimly as the anaconda's body writhed and whipped. The coil relaxed and Aqua was thrown out into the brush.

Hal went to the body of his friend and felt the heart. It was still.

He returned to the battle with the greatest of snakes. He was determined that Aqua should not have died in vain.

The head rope, passing through the cage and tied to a tree, was holding firm although it allowed far too much play. The tail rope had been caught now and lashed to another tree.

In vain the snake tried to capture more of its tormentors with its teeth or its tail. Hal got two Indians to help him haul in on the head rope. Every time the thrashing snake came nearer to the cage, it was held there until the next gyration brought it still nearer. Finally its head was in the door of the crate.

Its body was now almost straight, held taut by the tail rope. Hal ordered that this rope be slackened gradually as the head was drawn into the cage. The men worked with more confidence and courage as they saw that their enemy was being beaten. One of them even ventured to tie a rope to the snake's middle, and was knocked down twice in the process. By this rope the heavy body of the snake was drawn forward.

Finally the snake was in up to the full length of the cage. But there were still ten feet of snake outside!

The tail rope was now passed in through the cage and by means of it the tail was drawn in. The door was closed. The capture was complete.

Hal took no pleasure in it. It had cost too much. He took off his torn shirt, soaked it in the bay, and wiped the blood from Aqua's face. He had grown to be very fond of the able, intelligent and good-hearted young Indian. He felt that he and Roger had lost their most loyal friend.

Somehow the future seemed dark and dangerous, now that Aqua was gone.

The men carried the cage and its captive on board and half-filled the tub with water.

At dusk they buried Aqua under the tree where he had given his life.

265

24
Nine Headless Men

On down the river. It was no fun now. Hal could think only of reaching Manaos, getting his collection on board a steamer, and sailing home.

The jungle had become a place of death and terror. He had a sinking feeling that there was more trouble ahead.

To make matters worse, Roger had come down with fever. He had been too careless about taking his daily dose of malaria-preventing atebrin and keeping his mosquito net closely drawn around his hammock at night.

He lay in the toldo of the montaria with the boa constrictor and a few other animals to keep him company.

Hal had begun to hope that they were rid of Croc; but one day he heard war drums beating and, as his fleet rounded a point, he saw an Indian village on fire. That looked like Croc's work. He felt sure of it when he saw Croc's boat drawn up on the beach.

Hal did not feel able to interfere. With Roger sick and Aqua gone he could not fight Croc's gang. He hoped only that he could get by without being seen.

Some five miles farther downstream he pulled in for the night to a sheltered landing place behind a point.

As the men made camp, they stopped every few moments to listen. The drums of the burned village could still be heard. The rhythm was taken up by other drums behind the camp and downstream, and then in unseen villages on the other side of the river. The whole forest seemed to throb with the threat of the drums.

Hal's men were very nervous. They huddled together and whispered. Banco seemed to be stirring them up. Hal walked over to the group.

"What's the matter, Banco?"

"The drums, *senhor*. The men are afraid of the drums."

"Why are they afraid? Indians would not hurt Indians."

"They are not of the same tribe. The Indians in this forest are very savage. They hate the white man. Perhaps white men have attacked them today. They seek revenge. If they find you they will kill you, and all who serve you."

Hal laughed. "I don't think it's as bad as you make out, Banco." Many times on the trip he had noticed that Banco's liver was pretty white.

The men had gone out on the cape and were jabbering excitedly and pointing upstream. Hal joined them.

Against a red sunset the smoke of the destroyed village rose into the sky. But it was not this that attracted the attention of the men. A boat was coming downstream. Hal could count nine men in it, but not one of them was paddling.

In fact, they did not move at all. They might as well have been sacks of meal. No sound of conversation came across the water.

A chill began to creep through Hal's veins. He noticed that a strange terror had gripped his own men.

Again he studied the men in the boat. They were much closer now. Still they did not move. Hal strained his eyes in the failing light. He could see no heads on the men. Of course he would see them in a moment. Every man had to have a head.

The current carried the boat within fifty feet of the point. Banco screamed like a woman. Hal had to believe it now. Nine headless men sat in the boat. Their size and their bloodstained shirts made it plain that they were not Indians.

They must be Croc's cut-throats, their own throats now cut by the vengeful Indians whose goods they had tried to steal and whose village they had fired. Then the Indians had arranged this gruesome exhibit and sent it downstream as a warning to all and sundry.

Along with his horror, Hal felt a vague sense of relief. This must mean that he no longer needed to fear Croc. As for the Indians, he had never yet found any reason to fear them if they were treated fairly.

He went back to the camp site and strung up his hammock and Roger's. There was no camp fire that night.

The men usually slept on shore but tonight they preferred to lie in the montaria. To make more room for themselves they transferred what few animals it contained to the Ark.

Roger was always dead to the world when asleep and Hal, thoroughly tired, slept soundly in spite of the drums. Once, half awake, he thought there was a slight commotion on the montaria – then he slept again.

25
Deserted

Hal was awakened by the sun in his face. He stretched lazily, put his arm over his eyes, and rested.

He always enjoyed these few moments in the morning – lying at ease, listening to other men work. The Indians would be gathering fuel for the fire. It would be a little difficult, for there had been rain during the night. The water still dripped from the strip of canvas stretched above Hal's hammock.

There would be the chatter of Indian voices, the clatter

of pans, the smell of woodsmoke, and then the smell of coffee.

But all this ought to be already going on. The men usually turned out just before sunrise. He could hear nothing – nothing but the ordinary forest sounds and the continued angry mutter of Indian drums.

He uncovered his eyes and looked out into the camp site where a breakfast of turtle's eggs, baked curassow, and coffee ought to be on the fire.

There was no one in the camp site.

This would not do. The men were getting lazy. He would soon fix that. Hal climbed from his hammock and pushed out into the clearing. He started for the montaria which had been moored close to the beach.

Then he stopped, puzzled. The montaria was gone.

The fear of the future that had come to him when Aqua was killed flooded back upon him. But perhaps the men had just gone fishing.

He knew he was fooling himself. They would not all have gone – some would have stayed to attend to the morning fire.

He went out on the point. He could see far downstream and up. There was no boat.

There was no use kidding himself. His crew, fearing the

271

wrath of the local tribes, had set out for home. He could thank Banco for this. Only Banco could have persuaded them to abandon two boys in the jungle.

They had taken his boat. He had to admit that this was fair enough, for he owed them money. But probably they had also stolen everything else they could lay their hands on.

He went back to the bay and boarded the Ark. At least they had not made off with that. The animals had not been touched and they joined in demanding breakfast. Hal examined the supplies, nets, fishing gear, canned foods, valuable papers, medicines, guns, and ammunition. Not a thing had been touched.

That was to the credit of his crew. But it did not change the fact that he and Roger were now alone against the jungle – and Roger lay helpless in his hammock. The Indians were on the warpath. Hal thought of the gruesome sight of the evening before. It was not hard to imagine that soon two more headless bodies might be floating down the Amazon.

He heard a faint call from Roger. He took the boy a drink of water and his morning dose of quinine. Roger's forehead was very hot. Hal told him what had happened.

Roger was too sick to care. His mind wandered a little

and he did not quite grasp what Hal told him.

"Why can't you let me sleep?" he said peevishly.

Hal let him sleep while he went to get something together for breakfast. He found himself making all his movements to the rhythm of the drums. Would those drums never stop?

He gave Roger a spoon-fed meal of eggs and coffee. Then he took his rifle and went out to find food for some of his animals – especially the anaconda, which was too restless for the good of its cage. It had whipped all the water out of its tank. There was no use putting in more until the snake was satisfied. Then it might lie still.

Hal followed the shore downstream, hoping to find an animal coming to the river to drink.

Suddenly he saw, to his great astonishment, what he took to be an Indian standing waist deep in the water and, beside him, an Indian woman with a child in her arms. Another look, and he realized that these were not Indians. As he came closer he could make out their tiny slits of eyes, blunt noses, and thick lips.

Sailors in tropical seas had often been fooled just as Hal had been. Many a sea-going man had sworn that he had seen a creature with the body of a woman and the tail of a fish sitting on a rock combing her hair or suckling her child. Possibly it was in this way that the legend of the mermaid had begun.

But at close range Hal saw that this madonna of the Amazon had none of the beauty we like to think of as belonging to the mermaid. Her face and that of her gentleman friend were as homely as the face of a cow. And Hal knew that he was looking at the sea cow, the manatee, or, as the Brazilians call it, the fish ox.

There they sat on their tails among the weeds, the female feeding her baby, the male nibbling at water lilies, their erect bodies swaying slightly in the swell that came in from the Amazon.

What mammoths they were! If the parts concealed by the water were in proportion to the parts he could see, each of the animals must be at least ten feet long and weigh a ton. He could not undertake to deliver one of these to the anaconda.

Then a splashing of flippers drew his attention to another member of the family. It was a youngster perhaps five feet long and probably weighing not more than fifteen stone – just a fair snack for the big reptile. It was floundering about in a few inches of water, feeding on the grasses that grew along the bank.

Hal fired. At the sound, the two large heads immediately

sank out of sight. But the young manatee began to beat clumsily with flippers and tail in the shallow water. Hal came closer and fired again. He was thankful that he had a .300 in his hands, for he knew that the hide of a manatee is so tough that the Indians make shields of it.

The sea cow slowly bumbled itself around, but before it could get started towards deep water Hal had it by the tail. He did not attempt to carry it overland. Letting the water support its weight, he pulled it through the shallows until he got it alongside the Ark. Then he heaved the head up until it rested upon the gunwale and teetered it there, inching the body higher until it flopped over into the boat.

The hide was slippery enough so that he could drag the big animal to the door of the snake's cage. Now came the ticklish part of the performance.

How was he going to get the heavy "fish ox" into the cage without letting the anaconda out?

The snake was very active this morning. It kept striking its big head against the door of the cage. It lay with its thirty feet of length doubled so that the end of the tail was also near the door. Both the head and the tail were dangerous.

Hal had no fear of snakes, ordinarily. He had handled many kinds, from water moccasins to big Rocky Mountain rattlers. But he could never look at this giant of the snake world without a quivering of his nerves.

It was not just that the serpent was so huge. It was mean. No one had ever been able to make friends with an anaconda. In this respect it was quite different from the sweet-tempered boa constrictor, which might be made a household pet and become as affectionate as a dog or cat. The anaconda was the gangster of snakedom. He was on bad terms with everything and everybody.

And Hal knew that the moment he opened that door, jaws like a steel trap would close on his leg and that anxious tail would whip around his body.

The baby tapir came up to nuzzle its long nose against him. The big snake glared at it hungrily, then drew back its head and shot it forward with terrific strength against the door of the cage.

Hal picked up the tapir and carried it down the side of the cage to the other end. The anaconda's head followed. Hal tethered the little animal within a few feet of the bars. The evil eyes that seemed so hypnotic were fixed upon it. But the tapir, thanks to being very near-sighted, was not disturbed.

Hal went back to the cage door. He still did not dare to take the time to ease the manatee through the door,

276

for the snake might wheel about before he was half done. He studied the manatee. Its flat, paddlelike tail gave him an idea.

He tied a stout rope around the door and the door jamb so that the door would open only two inches. Then he pushed the flat tail of the manatee through this crack.

He went and got the tapir and brought it back near the door. The snake followed and discovered the appetizing tail of the sea cow. The serpent's jaws immediately locked themselves upon it and began to draw it in.

Once a snake has begun a meal it thinks of nothing but to finish it. Hal eased the rope so that the door opened wider and wider to admit more and more of the great walrus-like mammal as the snake sucked it down. When the whole manatee was within the cage, and half of it within the reptile as well, Hal could close and lock the door.

"There," he said with satisfaction. "Digesting that will keep you out of mischief for a few weeks at least."

He was sorry in a way to see so strange a mammal that would have attracted so much attention in a zoo disappear down a snake's throat. But he knew that no aquarium outside of the tropics has been able to keep a manatee alive for more than a few months. Probably it would not even have lived until he could get it home.

He went foraging again for his other animals. Just keeping this menagerie fed was a full-time job. He missed Roger's able help. And a burden seemed to settle upon him as he thought of undertaking singlehanded to sail his floating zoo down river.

There was just one silver lining – he no longer had to worry about Croc and his gang. Or did he? Were they all dead? He had never known exactly how many men there were in Croc's party. On the night of the attack he had estimated the number at eight or ten. There had been nine headless men in the boat – surely that was the entire band. And yet he was haunted by the uneasy feeling that Croc might still be alive. It was a daytime nightmare that kept nagging him. He tried to laugh it off, but it was not easy to laugh, alone and deserted, in a dark and sinister jungle. Men had been known to go mad in the terrible loneliness of this black forest.

And so he was quite willing to believe that he was touched in the head when he saw Croc stumbling towards him through the gloom. There was no mistaking him – the only other face like that was a vampire bat's. And even that was an insult to the vampire. The man's shirt and trousers were bloody and torn. His hair was unkempt, his face scratched by underbrush and haggard with sleeplessness and terror.

He stopped and stared at Hal. Then he came on with a rush. Hal raised his gun. He lowered it again when he saw that Croc was not armed. Croc collapsed at his feet.

"Buddy, am I glad to see you!" he whined. "Don't let them, buddy. Don't let them get me." He threw his arms around Hal's leg and sobbed, "They'll kill me, buddy. That's what they'll do. They'll kill me."

"And a good job too," said Hal, kicking the man off. "Don't you think it's a little strange to come to me for help?"

"Listen, buddy, listen," wailed Croc. "We're white men, ain't we? We white men have got to stick together. You won't let those dagoes get me?"

"Did you fire that village?"

"Oh that — that was a mistake."

"Did you kill any Indians?"

"Not many. What's a few Indians?" He slowly got up and looked behind him, still trembling. "They're after me. Where's your camp, buddy?"

Hal looked him over for a long minute. How he would enjoy filling this skunk with lead! He ought to give the cringing cur a kick and send him out into the jungle to die or be captured by Indians.

He turned and led the way to the camp. Croc, as big

and shambling as a giant anteater, shuffled along beside him. "God'll bless you for this, buddy," he croaked. "I knew you couldn't leave a white man in this beastly jungle. You and me is going to be friends, eh buddy? Best of friends. Everything forgotten and forgiven, ain't that right? That's the spirit."

He pulled up short as they came out into the camp site. "Where's your men?"

"Gone up river."

"Cripes! That's the way with them Indians. Never can trust them. Did you lose your animals too?"

"No. They're in the batalao, just around the bend."

"Fine!" Croc said with enthusiasm. "Buddy, you're in luck. Just when you lose your men I come along. You can depend upon me. I'll help you get that boat down river. Least I can do. Got anything to eat, buddy? I ain't eaten for twenty-four hours."

Hal fed the man.

"Where's your brother?" asked Croc. "Out gunning for game?"

"No. Back there in his hammock. Fever."

"Ain't that just too bad. You really *are* alone, aren't you?"

Hal glanced at him sharply. "I'm alone, but that doesn't mean that you can try any tricks. You're alone too. We saw your friends go by last night. How did you escape? I'll bet you were hiding in the bushes while they were fighting."

"What's the use of having men if you don't make 'em fight for you? Now, let's not get to arguing. Let's be done with feudin'. Sort of thing I been through sobers a man up. I made up my mind back there in the jungle that if the good Lord would just bring me out safe I'd never touch a hair of any man's head again. I'd be as gentle as a lamb. That's the way I says it to myself – gentle as a lamb. I wouldn't hurt nobody, no matter what I was paid to do it. I tell you, when you get to where any minute may be your last, you change your mind about a lot of things. And when I saw you – I couldn't 'a' been gladder to see my own brother." He helped himself to another large piece of dried meat. "Yes, sir, that's what we'll be, brothers."

"Like Abel and Cain," said Hal, but Croc did not catch his meaning.

"Just like brothers," he repeated. He looked out across the Amazon. Hal followed his gaze. The water was higher than the day before and the current past the point was more swift. An uprooted tree drifted by. Floating islands, always to be seen in the Amazon, were more frequent now. They were signs of the coming of the great annual flood.

"Must be heavy rains up river," Croc said. "A week from now right here where we're sitting will be under water. Chunks of dirt big enough to build a house on will be floating down. And them drifting trees can stave in a boat without trying. But don't you worry – we'll put your craft safe into Manaos before things get too bad. Lucky I came along. Leave it to me, buddy." He stood up, grinned his ugly grin and thumped himself bravely on the chest.

An arrow whizzed past him and struck a tree. Croc was in the bushes in a trice. Hal could hear him running heavily through the underbrush.

Roger called weakly from his hammock, "What's up?"

"Lie low," Hal warned. "Indians."

He advanced in the direction from which the arrow had come. "We are friends!" he shouted in the *lingua geral*, the general language of the Indians.

The answer he got was another arrow, barely missing his shoulder.

He thought of the nine headless men and of Roger lying helpless in his hammock. The best way to defend Roger would be to carry the fight away from him, up into the woods. He ran forward. His gun was ready. If they would not accept friendship they would have to take bullets.

As he broke into the jungle another arrow sang by. He thought it strange that the arrows always came singly.

Then he saw the reason — there was just one Indian. Upon seeing that he was pursued by a man with a gun, he turned and fled. Hal followed him for about half a mile. The Indian was too fleet for him and finally disappeared in the direction of the burned village.

He was doubtless a scout. He would come back with all the warriors of the village. Hal ran back to camp. There was no time to be lost. He and Roger and their unwelcome guest must board the Ark at once and be off.

He stripped down the hammocks and carried them and Roger's heavy, half-conscious form through the underbrush to the shore of the bay. He had not had time to think of Croc. Now he felt a cold dread of what he might discover when he came out on the beach.

He burst from the thick screen of leaves into the sunshine, and halted. It was true then. A man really could be capable of sailing off and leaving two boys at the mercy of the jungle, and of hostile Indians. The Ark did not lie moored near the beach.

Far out in the river the Ark sped downstream under full sail aided by a powerful current. Croc had nothing to do but steer. He stood on the steering platform at the stern with his hand on the tiller. He waved his other hand and his harsh voice came distantly across the water.

"So long, buddy. See you in hell!"

26
The Floating Island

Hal raised his gun. He lowered it again – the range was too great. Besides he remembered that he had only one cartridge left. That one had Croc's name on it. Somehow he would catch up with that devil and bore a hole clear through his evil carcass.

As he calmed down he realized that his chances of ever seeing Croc again were slim.

He laid Roger on the sand and began to take stock of the situation. He had no boat. He had no tools to make one. He had his hunting knife and, given a week, he might whittle out a raft. He was given not a week, but only minutes, an hour or so at the most. The scout might not have had to go all the way back to his village to contact his band. The Indians had been hunting Croc and might be very near by.

He and Roger might hide in the jungle. But they had none of the things they would need. He had stowed everything on the Ark in preparation for sailing. Even the pans he had used to get breakfast were on board.

He took an inventory. Between them they had two

shirts, two pairs of trousers, two pairs of alpargata sandals, two hammocks, one knife, one gun with one bullet – and that one bullet reserved.

Nor was the jungle a good hiding place. From white men perhaps. But not from Indians. The enraged Indians scouring the forest in search of Croc would find them sooner or later.

And the greatest objection to hiding out in the woods was that it would not bring him any closer to Croc. As he watched the black speck of the Ark disappearing down river it seemed futile to hope to bring Croc to a reckoning, or to recover his collection.

That was the worst of it – losing the animals. That meant failure for his father's business and victory for Shark Sands and his henchmen. It meant, too, that Hal would not get the chance to go to the South Seas – the reward that had been offered by his father for success in the Amazon enterprise. But he was not ready to give up yet.

His roving eye lit upon a floating island passing the mouth of the bay. A wild thought came to him. He did not to stop to analyse it – there was no time to weigh chances. He lifted Roger and made his way out to the end of the point.

The river was browner, more turbid, and more rapid

than usual. The main current boiled past close to the point. Something colossal must be going on in the headwaters on the flanks of the Andes. The swollen river was dotted with moving islands. They were of different kinds, although all due to the same cause – flood.

One that passed very close was a kind that he did not care to trust – a bed of water hyacinths torn loose from some marsh. Only the leaves and flowers showed above the surface. Below, the bulbs must be tangled together in a tightly-knit mass. But the whole mat was not more than a foot thick and might not support two husky boys. Even if it did, one of those great floating trees with branches milling around like paddle wheels, and roots projecting like the tentacles of an octopus, might roll over the islet, destroying it and everyone who happened to be on it. Many boats, even large steamers, had been stove in by those crazily thrashing trees.

Then there were islands made up of brush. In some rapids a bush had caught on a rock. Other bushes, sticks and logs had joined it, and the whole had been matted firmly in one solid mass and had finally broken loose to sail downstream as an island – an island without soil.

But more amazing were the islands that had soil, plants, even trees – everything an island should have except the

287

ability to stay in one place. A strong current had undercut a piece of land and carried it off entire. Some of these islands were two hundred feet across. He had heard that they were at times twenty feet thick.

But Hal could not wait for the ideal island – he must take the first reasonable chance that came along. He explained his purpose to Roger who only half-understood what it was all about. Something that looked like a large pasture came floating down and when it grazed the point Hal stepped aboard with his burden. He was thankful that he did not immediately sink through into the river.

In a moment the point was left behind and the two boys were embarked upon as strange a voyage as anyone had ever made.

Perhaps it had been a crazy idea. But anything was better, Hal told himself, than sitting on shore waiting to be beheaded. Now they were leaving behind those eternally thumping, nerve-wearing drums. And he was on the trail of Croc.

True, Croc could go faster with a sail than he could on a floating island. But suppose the wind dropped, or veered to blow upstream. Suppose Croc got caught on a sandbar or on a sunken log. Lots of things might happen to delay him. Hal considered that he had a fighting chance.

He surveyed his floating kingdom. He laid Roger down in the grass and walked about, frequently testing the ground to be sure that it was strong enough to hold him. His island was a good half acre in size. Much of it was in grass but there were also many small trees, especially cecropias, rubber trees and bamboos. The fast-growing bamboo was tall but all the other trees were not more than a few feet high.

Hal's active mind went to work on this curious fact and he came out with what he believed to be the answer. His island was quite evidently only a year old. The flood of a year ago had deposited a half acre of silt somewhere and, when the water subsided, there was a new island. Seeds sprouted and trees attained a year's growth. And now comes this year's flood to undercut the island, lift it from its firm base, and carry it off bodily down river.

The only trouble with his theory was the fact that on the downstream side of the island lay an enormous tree that must have taken a hundred years to grow. He walked over to examine it. It was a great silk-cotton, or kapok tree. Its trunk lay in the water and its huge branches rose some fifty feet into the air. At the base of the trunk was a tangle of big roots.

No, his theory still held water. This tree was not a part

of the island. The two had merely become jammed together while floating down river.

But he could use the fallen giant to good advantage. He strung up the hammocks between the branches, then brought Roger and laid him in his hammock where he would not be in danger from snakes or army ants or any other wild life there might be on this little floating world.

Which reminded him that he must feed his patient and himself. That was a sobering thought. Many an adventurer in the Amazon forests had died of hunger even though he had the entire jungle to draw upon. Hal had only the resources of a half acre. Robinson Crusoe had had much more to work with.

Hal spent the rest of the day having bright ideas that didn't work out. He looked among the bamboos for shoots, but there were none small enough to be edible. He tried the berries on a bush, only to make himself sick. He saw a little tree which he believed to be the famous cow tree which, when slashed, gives forth a very good substitute for cow's milk. He slashed this one but it was too small – only a few white drops exuded.

This was proving more of a job than he had expected. Once he had read the Fighting Forces Handbook, *Survival*, and had derived from it the idea that survival whether in the jungle, in the Arctic, in the desert or at sea, was really a simple matter. It did not appear so simple now.

But there must be plenty of fish in the river. He had no line – but he would catch them as the Indians did. He spent two hours fashioning a wooden spear with a barbed point. Then he went to the edge and looked down into the swirling current.

He soon realized that he had wasted his time. The current was so full of silt that he could not see one inch into its depths.

A heavy squall came up and Hal was promptly drenched to the skin. He didn't mind that. But after the rain came a strong wind, with nothing to stop its sweep across the great river, here eight or nine miles wide. Hal began to shake in his wet clothes and long for the shelter of the forest. It was hard to believe that he was within four degrees of the equator.

He continued his vain quest for food until dark. As night closed in, he made his brother as comfortable as possible. Fortunately Roger had been protected from the rain by the canvas over his hammock.

Hal would have liked the cheer and warmth of a camp fire. But there were two good reasons for not making a fire: (1) the Indians might see it; (2) the matches were on the Ark.

So Hal, quite forlorn and miserable, and humiliated by his failure to find food, crawled into his hammock. He was discovering how grim the Amazon can be to those who meet it unprepared.

There was something a little terrifying about barging through the darkness at the mercy of a strong current. What if his hurrying half acre should crash into a point, or a fixed island? He tried to tell himself that it was not very likely. His craft was carried by the current, and the current goes around things, not into them. A lone Indian who wanted to travel night and day, but must get some sleep, would tie his canoe to a floating island and wake up in the morning to find himself some thirty miles further downstream.

It suddenly struck Hal that night travel gave him one great advantage over Croc. Croc would doubtless stop and camp every night. Knowing so little of the river, he would hardly sail it in the dark.

Hal listened to the jungle roar. Sometimes it was far away and he knew that they were miles from shore. Then it would grow louder and louder as they approached a cape or a large island, and die away as they left it behind.

Once as they brushed the shore, the thundering voice of a jaguar not fifty feet away raised the hair on his scalp. He prayed fervently that the beast had not stepped out upon the floating island.

The biggest scare of the night came when the island scraped over a sandbar and the tree, with its lower branches rubbing on the bottom, began to revolve like a millwheel. Hal had visions of being neatly drowned if the branches to which the hammocks were fastened rolled under. Before this could happen the tree was in deep water and righted itself.

Hal gave up the idea of getting any sleep. He had no sooner done so than he slept, and did not wake until the sun looked in on him.

He scanned the horizon for the Ark, but there was no sign of it.

A faint call came from Roger. Hal climbed through the tree to his brother's hammock. Roger, half asleep, was calling for a drink of water. Hal put his hand on the boy's forehead. The patient seemed a little better.

Roger opened his eyes. He looked about him dully for a moment – then his eyes popped as he saw the swift river and flying shoreline.

"Hey, what's going on? How did we get here? Where's the Ark?"

"I'm glad you're well enough to ask questions," Hal said, and told him all that had happened.

Roger tried to rise but gave it up. "I'm as weak as a cat. Say, how about some breakfast?"

"You really *are* better," said Hal with satisfaction. "But as for breakfast — I'm afraid there will be a slight delay. I'll see what I can do."

He went out into his half acre, determined to make it yield up food and water.

One dare not drink water straight from the river except at the risk of typhoid and dysentery. It must be boiled. But how to boil water without any pan or teakettle, and without any fire?

Then he saw his tea-kettle. A joint of bamboo would do the trick. He went to the clump of bamboos and selected one that would not be too hard to cut with his hunting knife. He cut just below one ring and about eight inches above it. At each ring was a partition closing off the hollow interior. So Hal now had a pot three inches in diameter and eight inches deep. If what he had read was true, this pot would not burn when filled with water and placed over a fire.

But how about the fire? The first thing to do was to gather together something that would burn. Everything he touched was wet with last night's rain and this morning's dew.

Then he thought of the tree in which they spent the night. He took off some of the seed pods, each about twice as large as a walnut. He broke open the shells and found plenty of dry, fluffy cotton, the kapok used for mattresses. This would do nicely as tinder.

Then he cut through the wet bark of the tree. Sure enough the inside layers were dry. There was a plentiful supply of this material, and he piled all he could use upon the tinder.

Now he needed only flint and steel and he could make a fire. The blade of his knife was steel — but he had no flint. A stone might do. He searched his half acre but found not a single stone. The truth is that stones are almost non-existent in the Amazon flood plain. So the flint-and-steel idea was no good.

Well, he would use the fire-thong method. Primitive man had made fire that way — so could he. He found a piece of dry rattan that would do as a thong. He planted a stick slantwise in the ground, slit the end of it, put a little tinder into the slit, and then set to work drawing the thong rapidly back and forth in contact with the tinder.

The friction should make the tinder break into flame. It didn't.

In the South Seas, where he hoped to go, the islanders used the "fire plough". A groove was made in a piece of dry wood and a stick was moved back and forth in the groove so fast that the wood dust broke into flame. Hal rubbed vigorously for half an hour. Nothing broke, except his patience.

He stood with his hands in his pockets, puzzling over the problem. His right hand toyed with something round and flat. He drew it out absent-mindedly and looked at it. It was a lens that he had removed from his camera when he had substituted a telephoto.

"That will do it!" he exulted, and held the lens so that the rays of the sun passed through it and came to a point upon the tinder. In two minutes he had a fire.

Roger smelled the smoke. "Lucky you had matches," he said.

"I didn't have any matches."

"Gee whiz, don't tell me you made a fire without matches! You're getting pretty smart. What did you do, use a fire drill?"

"No," admitted Hal. "A Bausch and Lomb Tessar f 4.5. Afraid I'm not such a hot woodsman."

"Never mind," said Roger. "I'm betting on you."

Hal boiled the water, cooled it, and he and Roger drank.

But they were both hungry. Hal tried plaiting a fishline from grasses, but they broke. Then he discovered a rough piece of driftwood caught on the fringe of the island. Fibres like coarse hair clung to it. It must be the trunk of a piassava tree. This fibre was sold to North America and Europe to be made into brooms and brushes, ropes and cables. If it was good enough for that, surely it would do for a fishline.

While Hal was at work on the line he heard a chattering sound and looked up. A monkey looked down at him from a branch of the tree. Hal seized the weapon that had proved so useless in spearing fish and threw it in approved Indian fashion. It speared the monkey, which fell into Hal's hands. This was luck.

He postponed completing the fishline and immediately skinned the monkey. He laid aside some bones that would make good fish-hooks. He kept also a number of sinews. They could be used as leaders to fasten the hooks to the line. Then he roasted the monkey over the fire and breakfast was served. The fact that the time was nearly noon made the breakfast only more delicious.

Hal finished his line, attached a monkey-bone hook by a monkey sinew, fastened on monkey's knuckle bones as weights, baited the hook with monkey meat, and began to fish.

Presently he felt a strong tug on the line and he had immediately prospects of a fish dinner. He pulled up the fish and was astonished to find that it was only a few inches long. He was still more surprised when, upon grasping it to take it off the hook, it began to grow within his hand. It became too big for his hand, too big for both hands, and reached the size of a football.

He showed the curiosity to Roger. Roger tossed it against a branch and it bounced back like any well-behaved ball. Hal pierced it with the point of his hunting knife and it collapsed like a toy balloon.

"What's the idea of blowing itself up?"

"To frighten its enemies. Just the way a bird in a fight will fluff out its feathers, spread its wings, and raise its crest. Lots of animals act that way. It's animal nature and human nature. Plenty of men pretend to be bigger and more formidable than they really are."

He tossed the fish back into the water, knowing it to be poisonous.

His next catch put up a strong fight before he could get it out.

"It's a snake!" Roger exclaimed, as six feet of writhing fury rose into the air at the end of the line.

"An eel," Hal corrected.

But even Hal did not know that it was an eel of the electric variety until he took hold of it. He promptly let go again and slumped down in the grass, a violent pain coursing through every joint. The island faded out. When he came to, Roger was kneeling beside him.

"You scared me half to death," Roger said. "What struck you?"

Hal could not speak at once. He saw the eel lying in the grass. Roger was too close to it for safety. Hal tried to warn him, but the words would not come.

Roger, squatting on his heels, presently got his rear in contact with the eel. He brushed it only lightly and his trousers protected him, but nevertheless he went up into the air with a yell of pain. He didn't need to ask again what had struck Hal.

The paralysis disappeared gradually, but Hal's joints ached all the rest of the day.

With the true zeal of the collector, he resolved to take home this living storage battery. In the ground he dug a pit which filled with water. Using dry sticks, he pushed the eel into the pit.

"That will take care of it for the time being," he said.

He got Roger back into his hammock. The electric shock had not helped the convalescent.

"Too bad it isn't a cure for malaria," Hal said. "The Indians use it as treatment for rheumatism. And two of the big hospitals in North America send planes down here to collect electric eels for use in medical experiments."

"How much of a shock do you think you got from that thing?"

"I don't know. But they've measured the voltage and find that the average eel packs a wallop of three hundred volts."

"The bigger the eel, the bigger the wallop, I suppose."

"Not always. They tell of one eel only forty inches long that had an electromotive force of five hundred volts."

"Is that enough to kill you?"

"Well, perhaps not. But if you were in the water it would be enough to paralyse you so that you would drown. A good many cattle and horses have died that way. Humans too."

"If we ever get to the Ark, how are you going to carry this thing on board?"

"I've been wondering about that myself," Hal said thoughtfully. "Of course an electric eel doesn't have to shoot the works if he doesn't want to. The discharge is entirely voluntary. It's set off by a little trigger in his brain. It's just possible that if he were handled very, very gently he wouldn't turn on his dynamo."

"You'd be taking an awful chance."

"You're right." Hal's forehead kinked. "If I could just remember — I saw an electric eel taken apart one time in the Rockefeller laboratory. The thing that sets off the discharge is a nerve that runs all the way from the brain to the tip of the tail. If you cut that nerve anywhere, then only the part of the eel between that point and the head can shock you. You can take hold of the tail."

"And when you try this little experiment," said Roger, "be sure to give me a seat with a good view. That's something I want to see."

"No time like the present," said Hal, and he promptly staged the act. Taking his knife, which fortunately had a nonconductive wooden handle, he made a quick, light slash on the eel's back six inches forward of the tail. Then he touched the tail, and felt nothing. He took hold of it, lifted the eel into the air, and dropped it back into the pit.

"Operation successful."

Hal returned to his fishing and in due course pulled out a paiche. When he opened its mouth, several dozen tiny fish spilled out — for the paiche is the extraordinary fish that carries its young in its mouth. A very good precaution, thought Hal, in a river as full of voracious creatures as the Amazon. Particularly the dogfish loves to feed upon paiche small fry – and as soon as the dog-faced brute comes into the neighbourhood the little fellows make a dash for mother, who opens her capacious mouth to receive them. The big paiche made a very satisfactory evening meal.

The next day Hal saw a distant canoe and waved and shouted and even considered firing Croc's cartridge as a signal. The men in the canoe did not see the figure on the floating island.

Far more distressing was the event of the day following, when the Ark itself was sighted, moored to the shore. The island serenely sailed by it at a distance of a mile. Hal might possibly have swum to it in spite of a river full of teeth, but Roger certainly could not. There was nothing to do but sail on.

Croc was not visible – possibly he was in the woods foraging for the menagerie. How would he know what to feed the animals? If Hal did not get back to them soon, half of them would be dead. Or suppose Croc did know how to take care of them? Suppose he got them safely to Manaos and on board a steamer and away? Suppose Hal had to go home empty-handed?

Once you started supposing it was hard to stop. Suppose

he, too, came down with fever, by turns delirious and unconscious, and they both lay helpless in their hammocks until one of the terrific squalls for which the rainy season was famous broke up their island or rolled the tree over and fed them to the fishes.

The next morning Hal awoke to find that his island home was no longer travelling. At least, it was not travelling downstream. It had washed into a bay, and a back eddy was slowly carrying it round and round.

This was maddening. The Ark under full sail would speed by and be lost to him while he doddered around this bay. Every time the floating island came to the mouth of the bay he tried to pole or paddle it out into the main stream, but it was far too big a ship for one sailor to manage. The wind was upstream this morning and exerted just enough pressure on the high branches of the tree to push the mass back into the bay for another round.

Then Hal, looking up river, saw the Ark. It was not under sail. That surprised him – then the reason occurred to him. The same upriver wind that had pushed the island into the bay was making it impossible for Croc to use his sail. The Ark merely drifted with the current.

Hal had a sudden hope. If the wind had eased the drifting island out of the main current and into the bay, why shouldn't it have the same effect upon the drifting boat? Perhaps Croc would be joining him in a few minutes.

He prepared to receive him. He examined his Savage with a grim smile. Then he climbed into the tree and coached Roger.

"Lie still," he said, "and keep quiet."

Roger promptly climbed out of his hammock. "I'm sick of that thing anyhow," he said, wobbling a little as he hung onto a branch. "If there's a fight, I'm going to be in it."

"What can you do?"

Roger's eyes flashed. "I don't know, but I can do something. That fellow is as big as two of you. You'll need me."

"All right, but keep out of sight among the branches. He might see these hammocks," and Hal took them down.

Current and wind were carrying the Ark straight into the mouth of the bay. Hal patted his Savage. He scanned the deck in search of Croc. Finally he saw him, lying on the deck, sound asleep.

The animals called in vain for breakfast. Hal could hear the little tapir's whinny, the deep grumble of the jaguars, the chittering of the tiny marmoset, and the voices of the several birds.

How good everything looked, including Charlie, the mummified head, swinging by his hair from the masthead.

The big stork was as wise and one-legged as ever. The little deer was beautiful. Hal even had affection to spare for the evil anaconda.

The Ark entered the bay and followed the circling island. Hal feared that they would go around indefinitely, a few rods apart. But the island did not float as swiftly as the Ark. The heavy half acre scraped now and then on the bottom or against the shore. The Ark gained upon it and presently was wedged against it.

"Here we go," whispered Hal. Roger carried the hammocks. Hal slipped to the pool and very gently lifted out the eel by the tail. The boys sneaked on board the Ark behind the toldo. Hal laid the eel on the deck. It lay there quietly, never being very active out of water.

With the deck of his boat once more under his feet, the world looked good to Hal. He looked with surprise at the gun in his hand. The lust to kill had gone out of him. His fists felt as if they could do all that was necessary. He laid the gun down.

He stepped around the corner of the toldo. He beamed upon Black Beauty, who returned his advances with a cold stare. He beamed upon the anaconda, which did not trouble to open an eye, being still occupied in digesting the manatee.

More cordial was the pet boa constrictor. She wriggled across the deck to Hal, who leaned to caress her upraised head.

Nosey, the tapir, nosed his leg, and Specs, the marmoset, scrambled up and inside his shirt. Hal took him out, petted him a moment, and put him aside. Inside his shirt might not be a safe place for a marmoset a few seconds from now.

Hal looked down at Croc. The giant lay on his back, his face twisted and ugly even in sleep. He wore one of Hal's holsters and in it was Hal's own revolver. Hal stooped, gently extracted the revolver, and laid it on the anaconda cage.

Then he gave Croc a smart kick in the ribs.

"Uh-uh!" Croc grunted like an annoyed jaguar. His face squirmed as if snakes moved under the skin. His eyes opened by just a crack – then snapped wide as he saw Hal.

He rolled over and came up on his feet all in one motion, slapping his hand to his holster. He found no gun.

He charged into Hal like a wild bull. Hal, although tall and heavy for his age, weighed a good six stone less than his opponent. He stepped aside and let the big fellow go crashing into the toldo. The yellow tiger snarled and the black one roared. The birds squawked.

Croc turned, but before he could throw his weight

forward he got the full impact of Hal's fist in his face. Every shred of muscle the boy could command was put into that blow. He expected to see Croc crumple up.

Croc hardly seemed to notice the blow and came on again. This time his big ham of a fist contacted Hal's forehead and sent him spinning across the deck. His hurtling body knocked the single prop from under the giant stork, which went screaming into the air to the full length of his fifty-foot line.

Before the boy could rise, Croc seized one of the long, heavy oars of the batalao and brought it down with a crash – but not upon Hal, who had rolled out of the way and was now between Croc's legs, trying to upset the monster. He might as well have tried to throw an elephant.

Croc kicked the wind out of him. But Hal rose unsteadily to his feet and came back into the fight. He threw himself upon Croc and backed him against the anaconda cage. Croc flailed out with his heavy right fist. Hal went flat on the deck.

A roar of savage laughter came from Croc. Then he saw the revolver on the cage roof. He seized it and stepped forward to end Hal's troubles.

Then a scream escaped him as he saw a sight so horrible that he would remember it the rest of his life. A great greenish serpent was whirling in the air and coming straight towards him.

Roger, gripping the electric eel by the tail, swung it around his head like a lasso. David with his slingshot never approached Goliath more boldly. The terrified Croc fired, he did not know where or at what.

Now the green–black coils were going around his neck, round and round. An excruciating pain shot through him. His big hulk dropped unconscious to the deck.

27
The Caged Man

Hal and Roger stood looking down at the fallen giant.
Hal was badly shaken up and his convalescent brother was
puffing after his bout of eel swinging.

"What do we do with him now?" panted Roger. "We've
got to do something quick before he comes to."

The electric eel, its good work nobly done, was ambling
slowly across the deck towards the water. Hal seized it by

the tail, opened the anaconda cage, and managed to get the eel inside.

"It can't hurt the big snake, nor vice versa. And that tub of water is just made to order for an eel."

"But what do we do with Croc? Tie him up?"

"He deserves something worse than that," Hal said. "It would give me great pleasure to scare the liver out of him. He has it coming to him."

Roger's mischief mill began to work. He looked back and forth from Croc to the cage.

"I wonder how he would like the world's scariest snake for a travelling companion!"

Hal chortled. "Fever has made you brilliant, my boy." They heaved and hoisted until they got the one big giant into the cage of the other. They closed and locked the door. Croc lay not in the water but on the cage floor beside the tub where it narrowed at the end. A foot away from his face was the head of the sleeping anaconda, its body in the tub. Around it swam languidly the hero of the recent encounter, the electric eel.

The colour had drained out of Croc's usually beef-red face. Hal could see no sign that the man still breathed. He began to wonder how he would explain Croc's death to the police at Manaos. If he and Roger sailed into that port with a corpse on board they would most certainly be held for murder. He prayed silently that his worst enemy would come to.

A shiver ran through Croc's big frame. He began to pant.

Then his big eyes opened and he saw within a foot of him a head bigger than his own and almost as ugly. In terror he jerked his own head back and brought it with a resounding crack against the wall of the cage.

He looked about him frantically, found that he was trapped, saw the two boys regarding him with interest. He clawed at the door. He bellowed to high heaven.

"Let me out! Open the door!"

"Better pipe down," Hal advised. "You'll wake your friend and then he'll swallow you."

Croc compressed his voice into a harsh whisper. "If I ever get out of here I'll murder you."

"I know it. That's why you're going to stay in."

Croc arched his body against the tub and tried to break out the wall. But the cage had been made strong enough to withstand all the lashings of the most powerful of serpents. Its three-inch-thick bamboo pillars creaked a little but held fast.

The anaconda's head moved slightly. Croc flattened

himself against the wall and his eyes bulged. Ignorant of snake ways, he could not know that an anaconda, no matter whether asleep or awake, is hardly dangerous when full of dinner. He burst into hysterical curses.

When he saw that he could not frighten his captors into releasing him, he changed his tune.

"Listen, boys, this joke has gone far enough. I know you're good boys. You wouldn't really leave me here to die."

"You left us to die," Hal reminded him.

"Now, buddy, you've got me all wrong. I just wanted to save your collection and your boat, see. Hasn't it all worked out good? The jungle is no place for a coupla boys. I had to take care of you, see."

"We'll take care of *you* now," was Hal's unfeeling reply. "Come on, Roger. We have work to do."

And leaving their prisoner to rage or blubber as he pleased, they went ashore to gather meat, blood, insects and leaves to suit the various tastes of their animals.

"This ought to be the last feeding before we get to Manaos," Hal said.

"Are we that close?"

"We should get there tomorrow, if we have a good wind."

Returning to the shore they found that the floating island had left the bay. That must mean that the contrary wind had died down. They fed the animals, then hauled in the anchor. The Ark also circled out of the bay and into the main stream of the Amazon. A slight breeze was drifting down river. Hal ran up the sail and took his place at the tiller. Roger, still weak from his bout with fever, stretched out on deck close to the cage containing the three devils.

Roger kept watch to see that none of them escaped. The noisiest of the three was Croc. He was mad with fear when the anaconda sleepily opened its eyes and regarded him, stretched its jaws apart in a great yawn, and went to sleep again.

Camp was made for the night on a grassy point, but Croc stayed in his cage. Dried meat was passed to him between the slats. The killer, now in dread of a greater killer than himself, spent an uneasy night. Which was quite unnecessary, for the serpent he so frantically feared slept profoundly.

In the middle of the next morning the water suddenly changed from brown to black. That meant that the Rio Negro, Black River, had joined the Amazon.

The course of the Ark was changed and they sailed ten

miles up the black stream to the great jungle city of Manaos.

At Manaos the Rio Negro is four miles wide. At other points it is fifteen miles wide. And yet it is merely a tributary to the Amazon.

Manaos, where men made fortunes during the great rubber boom, is a thousand miles from the Atlantic Ocean. And yet it is an ocean port, and the boys found its docks full of cargo steamers that had sailed from North America, England or Europe down the Atlantic and a thousand miles up the Amazon to reach this, the greatest city of the Amazon basin.

The Ark, which had seemed so large, looked small in comparison with these ocean liners. The boys made it fast to a pier under the towering stern of a ship from Glasgow. The animals and the savage human in the anaconda cage immediately attracted a curious crowd. Roger undertook to keep guard while Hal went into town to police headquarters.

He asked for and got an interview with the chief of police. He quaked inwardly lest the chief should refuse to believe his story. He was greatly relieved when that dignitary said, "We owe you a great debt, *senhor*. We have word of all this from up river. We have a charge of robbery and incendiarism against this man by one under the name of Pero Sousa, and also complaints from the Cocamas, who charge him with murder of twelve of their people. My officers will accompany you to your boat."

Croc was removed from his cage and taken into custody.

Hal then visited the steamship offices. The result was a contract to transport his collection home on the good ship *Sea Gull*, Captain Brig Harris, master.

And then to the cable office to report to their father the successful outcome of their venture.

The following morning they received his reply:

YOUR MOTHER AND I MUCH RELIEVED TO KNOW YOU ARE WELL CONGRATULATIONS ON A FINE JOB YOU WIN THE TRIP TO THE SOUTH SEAS WILL MEET YOU WHEN YOUR SHIP DOCKS

The next few days were busy ones. Crates had to be made for the animals that had not already been caged. The collection had to be insured – Hal estimated its value at £10,000. The cages had to be hoisted on board the *Sea Gull*. The good old Ark had to be sold. Food had to be stored for the collection during the voyage home.

But it all got done. And there were no happier boys in Brazil, or possibly in creation, than the two who stood at the rail as the *Sea Gull* pulled away from the piers of Manaos into the glossy black current of the Rio Negro. Behind them, in cages occupying half the fore-deck, squawked, growled and chattered their precious menagerie. The removal of Croc from the picture lifted a great weight from their shoulders. Six days down the Amazon and twelve up the Atlantic and they would have their collection safe home.

"And next year the South Seas!" exulted Roger.

"Where I want to capture an octopus," said Hal.

"And I want to go whaling."

"And I want to dive for pearls."

"And I want to get shipwrecked on a desert island!"

SOUTH SEA ADVENTURE

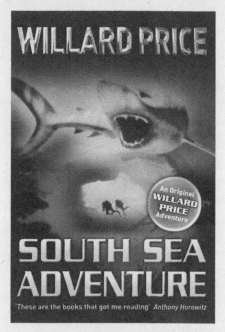

'It's a lost world out there . . .'

Hal and Roger Hunt sink deep into danger when a specimen-collecting trip takes them into the lost world of the South Seas. But the deep-sea trawl has a hidden agenda – a top secret mission for Professor Stuyvesant, and his scientific experiments in Pearl Lagoon . . .

ARCTIC
ADVENTURE

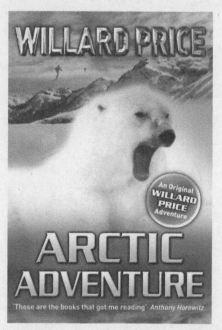

'Adrift in a savage land of ice and snow . . .'

Hal and Roger Hunt are colder than they've ever been in their lives, up among the ice floes of Greenland. This harsh land holds many dangers, from killer whales to grizzly bears, but an evil man may turn out to be the deadliest threat the boys have to face.

SAFARI ADVENTURE

'It's war. And right now we're losing it.'

Hal and Roger Hunt fly straight into the jaws of death when they join warden Mark Crosby in Tsavo, an African park where poaching is big business. And with a gang leaving behind a blood-stained trail of terror and torture, the heat is on for the brothers to solve the string of mysterious murders – before they too become victims . . .

ELEPHANT ADVENTURE

'You are walking into the jaws of death . . .'

Hal and Roger Hunt are on an awesome African adventure to track down the rare great white elephant. The brothers coolly tackle their task – despite doom-laden prophecies from Mumbo, a Watussi chieftain – and as the temperature rises . . . the danger level intensifies.

WILLARD PRICE

Willard Price was born in 1887 in Peterborough, Ontario. He had a special interest in natural history, ethnology and exploration and made numerous expeditions for the American Museum of Natural History and the National Geographic Society.

He went on to edit various magazines on travel and world affairs and spent six years working in Japan as foreign correspondent for New York and London newspapers. He wrote fourteen adventure stories featuring Hal and Roger Hunt. He died in 1983.